SEE HOW THEY RUN

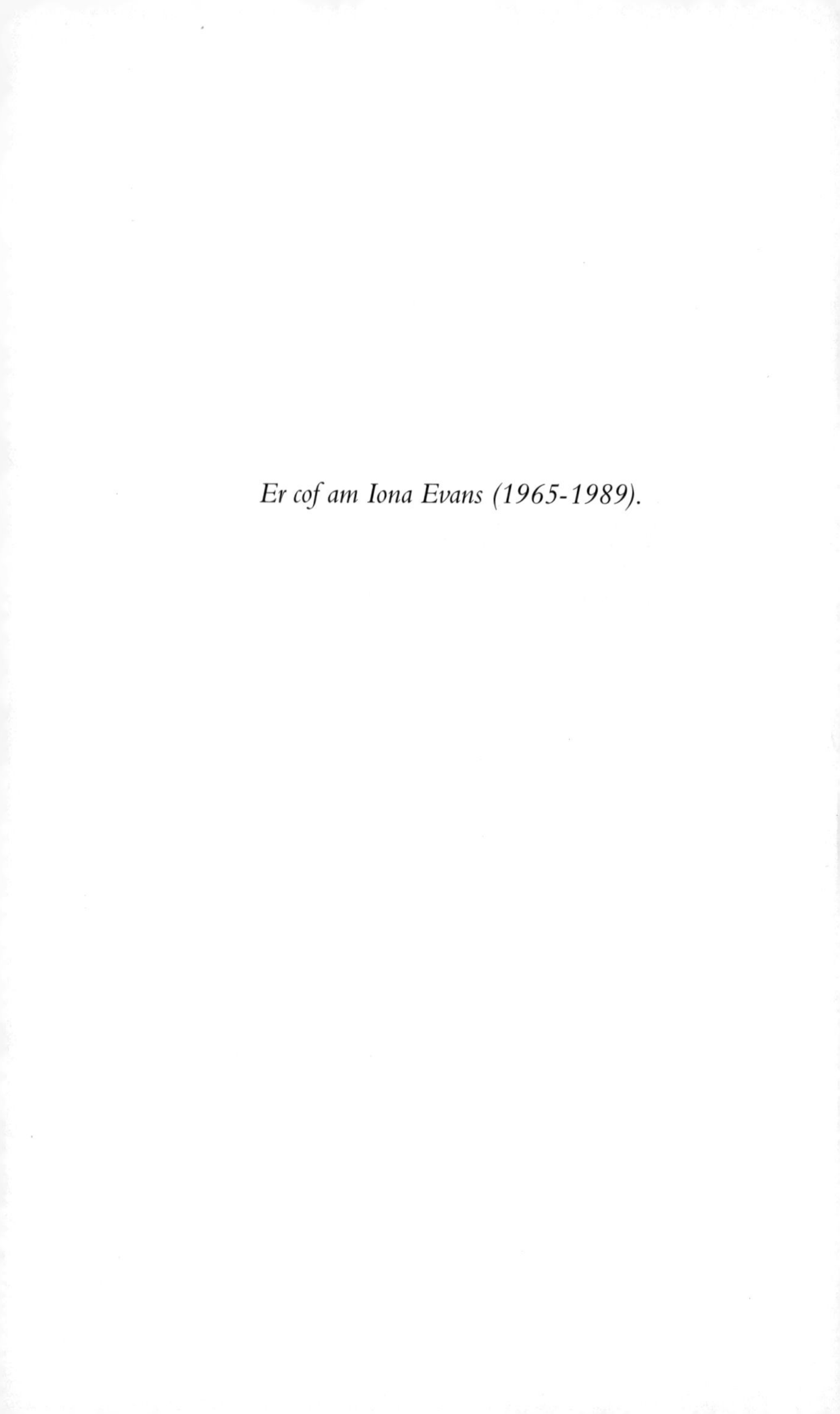

Er cof am Iona Evans (1965-1989).

LLOYD JONES

SEE HOW THEY RUN

NEW STORIES FROM THE

MABINOGION

SEREN

Seren is the book imprint of
Poetry Wales Press Ltd
57 Nolton Street, Bridgend, Wales, CF31 3AE
www.serenbooks.com

ISBN 978-1-85411-590-4

A CIP record for this title is available from the British Library.

Cover design by Mathew Bevan

Inner design and typesetting by books@lloydrobson.com

Printed in the Czech Republic by Akcent Media

The publisher acknowledges the financial support of the Welsh Books Council.

Contents

New Stories from the Mabinogion

Introduction

Some stories, it seems, just keep on going. Whatever you do to them, the words are still whispered abroad, a whistle in the reeds, a bird's song in your ear.

Every culture has its myths; many share ingredients with each other. Stir the pot, retell the tale and you draw out something new, a new flavour, a new meaning maybe. There's no one right version. Perhaps it's because myths were a way of describing our place in the world, of putting people and their search for meaning in a bigger picture, that they linger in our imagination.

The eleven stories of the *Mabinogion* ('story of youth') are diverse native Welsh tales taken from two medieval manuscripts. But their roots go back hundreds of years, through written fragments and the unwritten, storytelling tradition. They were first collected under this title, and translated into English, in the nineteenth century.

The *Mabinogion* brings us Celtic mythology, Arthurian romance, and a history of the Island of Britain seen through the eyes of medieval Wales – but tells tales that stretch way beyond the boundaries of contemporary Wales, just as the 'Welsh' part of this island once did: Welsh was once spoken as far north as Edinburgh. In one tale, the gigantic Bendigeidfran wears the crown of London, and his severed head is buried there, facing France, to protect the land from invaders.

There is enchantment and shape-shifting, conflict, peacemaking, love, betrayal. A wife conjured out of flowers is punished for unfaithfulness by being turned into an owl, Arthur and his knights chase a magical wild boar and its piglets from Ireland across south Wales to Cornwall, a prince changes places with the king of the underworld for a year...

Many of these myths are familiar in Wales, and some have filtered through into the wider British tradition, but others are little known beyond the Welsh border. In this series of New Stories from the Mabinogion the old tales are at the heart of the new, to be enjoyed wherever they are read.

Each author has chosen a story to reinvent and retell for their own reasons and in their own way: creating fresh, contemporary tales that speak to us as much of the world we know now as of times long gone.

Penny Thomas, series editor

See How They Run

I

He sat at his desk and felt really great. For the first time in ages: on top of his game. A strong surge of happiness had swept through him all morning; he felt clean, alert, and completely in control.

Good news had arrived in a steady trickle, as it does sometimes in life, and he felt really up for it. He enjoyed fresh starts, physically as well as mentally. They happened so seldom – they were rare and special. Anything was possible.

Today, on a Monday morning in spring, in his room overlooking the town, he studied his computer screen. He'd already changed the background to a shot he'd taken himself – a sheaf of young daffodils in the college grounds. Fresh start, fresh picture. Crisp and clear. It was almost religious the way he went about it; he could have been a hermit sweeping his cell on Christmas Eve, with a sprig of holly above the holy rood, his stone floor sprinkled with a dusting of fresh, windblown snow.

He fetched a hard drive from a low drawer to his right and, after connecting it, he filed away every single document and folder on the desktop, clearing the screen. Next he rearranged all the icons in a neat triple line on the left; then he played about with his recycle bin, before deciding to leave it in the bottom left-hand corner. The space to the right of the daffs was completely clear; when he leaned back in his chair to study the effect he felt a fresh surge of pleasure. A bright yellow light of optimism cheered the room. And outside, a neon sky. He'd studied it through his classical ogee window – a vast vault of blue, seemingly higher and broader than he'd ever seen it before. Looking out over the landscape he'd seen no movement at all, as if every single human had been transported somewhere else, leaving a virgin landscape. He tried to imagine the scene before modern history: a wide open country full of silence and measureless, limitless time. It was easier to imagine the deep past with a sad wind moaning outside. Using his imagination he could erase all the buildings below and travel swiftly backwards. That's why history had attracted him as a boy: as the wind saddened in the eaves of their rural cottage he had wondered about those lost, mysterious people toiling in their raw landscapes; he had been intrigued by their forgotten tombs and their uncontrollable myths.

Back in the present he toyed with the idea of binning the games folder, but he liked a quick bout of Solitaire or Mahjong Titans before he started, to limber up, so he stayed his hand.

There! He had a pristine desktop, and he went a step further, clearing his large pine desk of everything except for his fruit bowl and his regulation family photo, plus a new notebook and a new biro. He played about with their appearance on the desk, nudging each item in different directions until everything looked just right. Minimalistic and tidy. It was like being a god, rearranging the world. He was Zeus with a half-eaten apple in one hand and a mouse in the other, stooped over his computer, viewing the world within the screen, quietly planning, conniving, pushing his little playthings this way or that. He liked the image; he'd just finished a paper on the old Celtic gods, whose names no one knew, and his head was still full of them.

After storing the hard drive he rubbed his hand dry of apple juice and right-clicked a new folder into existence. It was neat the way he could do that. Sublime, creative. He labelled it *Notes* and filed away his first document, a memo from his head of department:

From: Professor M. Williams
To: all deans, faculty heads, everyone in the history department
Dr Llwyd McNamara has received a bursary to help him prepare a biography of the great rugby player Big M, and as a consequence he will take a term's sabbatical to research his project. Dr Fflur Ceiriog will take his lectures pro tem and I will take his seminars. I'm sure we all wish him

> well, and I look forward to reading more about this Welsh icon. An overview of the Irish tragedy is long overdue.

For years, Llwyd had used his unusual Christian name as a chat-up device during the seduction process, but since it was unpronounceable to most of the students, especially the large Chinese contingent who clogged his local Morrisons every term, he'd been secretly glad when the departmental secretary mutated it, though he felt she might have consulted him first.

So he became Lou to all except the small Welsh community at the college. Even his wife mocked him with it, gently and ironically. The Tibetans, she said, gave each child a new name if it survived a major illness. Was she implying something?

He'd never known why he had a Welsh forename. It was the only hint he'd been given regarding his paternity; his ma had refused steadfastly to tell him any more. He'd been born at a time when the only *special relationship* had been the bond between all the

Celtic countries, and not between a bunch of bent Americo-British politicians and their business cronies.

Llwyd meant *pale* and suggested a pasty, nerdy type. Even worse, it hinted at a furtive, malicious plotter, an Iago figure.

Lou positioned his new folder in the top right-hand corner and wondered if it looked right there, a small yellow bird in a big blue sky. Maybe he could customise it, and he toyed with the idea of phoning IT, but realised he wasn't sure what he wanted. A different colour maybe? He'd leave it for now. Perhaps one day there would be a whole department at the uni studying nothing else but computer iconography – a branch of semiotics, presumably. He'd like that, he was intrigued by symbols.

Next, he created another folder and labelled it *Ireland*. After moving it about with his mouse he finally positioned it directly below *Notes*. It was so agreeable, the way a folder glided into place when it was released by the mouse.

Finally, before starting on his fresh, daffodil-smelling project, he phoned Catrin to check up on her – because they'd both clicked another folder into being about three months previously; his partner was pregnant, and she was preparing that very day to set off to her parents' home in the hills to inform them.

It was going to be an exciting year, he could feel it in his marrow.

He celebrated with three straight clearances among the Mahjong Titans.

And yet something wasn't quite right. After winning his games he sat for a while, looking at the flatish bank of cumulus clouds he'd caught with his camera, above the daffodils, now frozen on his screen. He got up and went back to the window, finding another bank of clouds, lighter and longer, rumpled pillows drifting eastwards across the real horizon. In the doll-within-doll world of his computer the clouds had no emotional density; yet over there in the sky, moving very slowly in the far distance, they imparted a sensuous, supernatural otherness, a stratospheric mysticism; high in the blue above him they seemed to drift on the invisible winds of time, a fantastical convoy. He imagined the old deities sitting on their thrones of ether, drifting towards the edge of the world and the fringes of human comprehension. The clouds could also be seen as huge ships, Leviathan trawlers crawling with their engines merely ticking over, dredging the land; their cumulus shadows were long dark nets thrown out to gather the homesteads, animals, spinneys and churches below.

Lou considered the worlds within worlds around him: he himself had been hatched inside his grandmother, as an egg within his embryonic mother; now his genetic future was growing silently within Catrin, as a tiny cloud might form and gather at dawn below the sea's far horizon.

On his desktop lay a document within a folder within a computer within a room within a college within a nation, and so on ad infinitum – but almost everything he'd created so far had lain within the confines of academia. *Confines.* If he wanted to research this book properly he would have to leave the safety of his academic atoll, relinquish the beautiful digital shimmer inside the coral depths of his computer. He would have to step out into the real universe. The one with rain and death, not pretty icons and cursory games. Farewell to FreeCell and Mahjong Titans. Most of all he'd miss the pattern of books – a blow-up of scholarship's dusty butterfly wings – covering the entire wall to his right. Like the cloud-shadows dredging the landscape outside, his books had trapped him between the webbing of their printed lines and hauled him along the scholastic seabed. He'd been caught, hook, line and sinker.

By the end of the day, with Lou's customary efficiency, all the arrangements had been made. Ireland beckoned again. He hadn't been there for ages, not since his mother's funeral. This time he would call on another woman, whom he'd never met. He was slightly nervous about it. Lou had little experience of duplicity, but that's what he had in mind. Perfectly formed in his brain, like a cluster of anthers in one of his pixellated daffs, lay a series of acts which would bring him recognition and fame.

The train to Holyhead wasn't too bad, crowded but merry. Manly rolls of laughter, banter, heavy fried breakfasts still sludging through the pipes. But the ferry was packed, as you'd expect on a six nations weekend, and the close physical foreplay got on his nerves after a while so he went up alone on deck. He was with the usual college crowd, knowledgeable and experienced. They knew all about the game's mad frottage, its frothing convulsions; each scrum a huge spider silking its golden egg. And the three quarters all strung out, a line of fencing posts, wired in between with the blurred memory of a hundred thousand ancestral passes. Rugby was a war game to them, paintball with a pint in your hand. Up aloft in a nippy little wind he cowered in the lee of a stack and observed the glassy sea. He was having a problem with scale; his mind flickered to and fro. Here was hugeness, but all he could see was a miniature ferry crossing the screen of his computer, crossing a puddle by the daffs. Suddenly, he felt tiny. What did it mean: was he empathising with his embryonic baby, swimming in its own little ocean?

Or merely responding to the overpowering bulk of the mob around him? Who cared...

He shrank into his anorak and let his mind rove. He had always loved the sea, always felt completely at home either in it or on it. It was in his blood somewhere; maybe his forebears, his mother's kin, had been fishermen. Men like Tomas O'Crohan from the Great Blasket Island, who'd started every sentence with *yerra* or *wisha*. And didn't his surname have something to do with the sea? Didn't it mean *son of the hound of the sea*? The McNamaras had been warriors, apparently, building over fifty castles in Clare alone. Lou hadn't acquired the fighting gene but he was a fantastically good non-competitive swimmer, nicknamed *Sealboy* at school. And surely he was a true Piscean, never knowing whether to swim with the tide or against it.

The sea. Even today, standing above a holdful of semi-drunken urbanites at play, it was easy to imagine the Celtic world of prehistory; a seemingly endless body of water with distant shifts of light, soundless squalls at the furthest limits of seeing. A time when there was no land beyond the horizon, only water stretching to infinity. The world had been packaged and sold in lots since then; to the modern mind it was measured by the number of films you could see on a flight to New York; but once upon a time it was counted out in cubits and oar-lengths, and measured by the number of water-skins aboard a boat full of marauding psychopaths filling in their days between pillage and death. Dots on the faraway sea, the people of the old world were scarce and brave. What silence there must have been. And everyone a pilgrim. Just a few people, but a superabundance of ghosts and demons and spirits. Ship-devouring serpents and the hideous kraken. Mermaids and sirens. Every horizon was a knife edge, the rim of the cosmos.

It was all a matter of scale. But some things had remained the same. Mankind hadn't changed that much, only his playthings. Religion and superstition still abounded. Lou was a great toucher of wood and chucker of salt himself, he was as superstitious as the next man. Of course, his intellect had overridden all that stuff many years previously, but he still carried on with the rites. His superstition was nominal, he knew that; it was as virtual as the icons on his desktop, representing yet more representations.

Here he was again, alone on the planks of a boat. His ma had told him so many tall stories, he had no idea how many were true; her darling son was unique, she'd told him countless times at bedtime, tickling him and nuzzling her warm laughter into his neck, he was the only boy ever to be made *and* born on a boat in the middle of the ocean. So said his lovely freckly ma. His dancing-around-the-room ma, zany and boisterous, not the serious one who took him to church, or the ma who looked at his school report for far too long. Made and born at sea? Later, when he understood such things, he'd taken this to mean that he'd been conceived and delivered into the world on the Irish ferry, which wasn't as bonkers as it sounded, since she'd worked for Sealink as a stewardess. Broom cupboard love? Well, he'd never know now. As for his own love life, it had never been better. Catrin had bloomed during pregnancy and she was extra sexy all the time; he too had felt constantly aroused when he was anywhere near her. Completely normal, said the doctor. Now that Catrin was up the duff, all restraint had gone. *You lucky sod*, said the doctor's eyes. Hazel eyes, like his ma.

He was joined on deck for a while by a pretty young thing in a fluffy Welsh dragon hat, all legs and lipstick. She stood close to him in the diesel after-breath of the engines having a fag, and he felt a tug; his own rampant sexuality, ringing him in confident waves, had obviously reached her. He thought briefly about making a move but then she walked over to the rails and retched into the churning foam below. Charming, thought Lou, though he still unpeeled her banana-skin jeans with his eyes and ran his mind along her thighs.

Still completely and anomalously sober when they docked at Dun Laoghaire, he detached himself from his group, saying he'd see them later at the pub as arranged. They knew he had business.

The cab driver looked surprised and slightly pissed off when he said *Dalkley, please*. Too close maybe?

How could a man make a daysent penny? So the taximan took his time getting there, giving Lou a lingering view of Joyce's Martello tower. Soon they'd reached the town and Lou imagined Flann O'Brien's drunken weave along the pavement, Finbarr the King of Dalkey robed and resplendent in Finnegan's, enjoying the craic with Maeve Binchy, Bono and Enya, talking about fame and pilchards.

Lou had the address, somewhere grand on the Sorrento Heights, in his notepad and he pushed it through the gap between the seats. *Christ, how much would a place like that put you back*, said the driver when they got there. *You want me to wait, surr?*

His mock-respect was delivered with such panache that Lou replied *why not?*

His face must have shown surprise when she opened the door, but she didn't seem to notice. What had he expected? An academic widow in early middle age, slim, intelligent eyes, mouth of a madrigal singer? All the old platitudes? But she wasn't the wife he'd expected, clearly. She was the mother, as it turned out, a dowager queen from one of the old

Irish dynasties, freshly risen from a phantom levee, her mirthless grey eyes stripping him bare in moments. She was tall and straight, in a long black dress with a lace collar and cuffs, so ancient it could have hung in the V&A. She was Queen Medbh of Connacht at the ford, ready to gird Fergus for his bull raid. Or a brogue Miss Havisham maybe, severe and insane, trapped for ever in a huge decaying mansion, her clock stopped at the moment her son died. But far from being cobwebbed and dusty, the room in which they sat at opposite ends of a massive dining table was immaculate and set ready for a banquet: starched linen, gleaming glassware.

We always celebrate when we beat the Welsh, said her silhouette at the other end of the room. She sat bolt upright, shoulders held high, her hands placed magisterially in front of her, framing the fish fork and the soup spoon. A dinner service, hand-painted with the famous trellis shamrock, caught the fire of the sun on an adjacent table. Surely she knew all the old supper party songs: *Pale hands I loved, beside the Shalimar*; or maybe a John McCormack classic,

The harp that once through Tara's halls...

Behind her lapped the medieval sea which Gerald of Wales had seen, menaced by a giant whirlpool sucking at passing ships; behind them both lay the holy land of Ireland, stalked by Gerald's talking wolves, women with beards, wandering bells, vindictive saints, creatures which were half ox, half man; geese which hatched from barnacles growing on gum trees, and a rude, musical peasantry sustained by miracles and bestiality. The old, primitive shadows were still there, but vestigal now. Outside, framed by the window, he imagined an enormous pair of legs disappearing into the clouds. Huge knees, scarred and raw. He could smell the mossy, earthy leather of the house-sized cordovan boots; and waving slowly in the air, reminding him of seaweed moving with the tide, body hair as thick as jungle vines.

She gave him what he wanted, in the crystaline light of spring, a severe woman without any grief left to show, stripped of it, a bleached bone in a cyst.

Her son had collapsed suddenly during a lecture, clutching his left shoulder. Not yet fifty, her brilliant offspring had gone to the otherworld. Dr Dermot Feeney, who had risen from being a clerk in a shipping office, who had worked himself up from nowhere, had been too busy in his stone-lined study to beget a family, despite his mother's pleas. So Dermot Feeney, launched from this woman's thighs less than fifty years ago, had died intestate and without issue; his sole bequest a thick wad of paper containing his life's work, accompanied by a slender memory stick, also containing his life's work. A pencilled note had said: *In the event of my death, please deliver this to Dr Llwyd McNamara, requesting him to complete my book.* Taking the package from a drawer, she deposited it on the corner of the table near his right hand and went back to her seat. Feeney's magnum opus was now in Lou's sole possession; the note was still there on the cover, in a forward-slanting script; the man had been in a mighty hurry. Lou already imagined its scholarly pages drifting on the mid-channel breeze, heading one by one towards a soggy funeral in the Irish Sea. Poor silly pup, thought Lou, to entrust his work to a rival – his *biggest* rival. The memory stick, lizard green and semi-opaque, reminded him of his childhood swatch. It was rather beautiful, nicely proportioned, slightly sad. No manufacturer's name, merely a symbol showing radiating waves and the letters 4GB. The snap lid was pleasantly coved rather than straight, and the other end had an eyelet. Lou took it in the palm of his hand and admired it, a coffin of memories lying there. Someone else's memories; someone else's lifeblood in a fragment of plastic. Dimly, he could see its inner workings; rows of tiny components glinting like a canteen of silvery fish in a milky green sea. This was what he'd come for; another man's genius, so that he could destroy it. Dr Feeney had been his main rival in their chosen arena, the history of Celtic sport; Dr Feeney had also beaten him to it with a much-discussed but as-yet unpublished history of the Irish tragedy. It was vaunted as the definitive work on Big M, or *Your Man* as he was known in Ireland, the *Man* being a convenient shorthand for his perplexing middle name, Manawydan, passed on from father to son for countless generations before it lodged latterly between Dylan and Jones in a South Wales valley. The little lad had made a lot of noise as he came down the tunnel, but right from the start he'd looked every inch the famous second row forward he became. He'd come out with a headband and cauliflower ears, said the wags at the Miners Arms. The broken nose came later, on his first day at nursery school. So said the hairy little giants who propped up the bar at the Miners Arms. But they didn't know, back then, about the mouse tattoo; that titbit of news was still down a hole, waiting to be caught...

Lou backed out of this palace from the past as soon as decency allowed and escaped to Dublin, thrusting the package into his backpack, a washed-out old Karrimor inherited from his ma. He zipped the memory stick into his anorak's inner pocket. When they reached Doheny and Nesbitt's in Lower Baggot Street he was stung for a rake of cash by the taximan, and he started to haggle on the pavement, but gave up immediately when the man got out and stretched to his full length, leaning towards him with his huge elbows on the roof of the car. Lou was a sensible man or a coward; he'd not decided which yet.

The pub was packed, already stir crazy, and most of his colleagues were steaming. He tried to catch up with them by downing a few double whiskeys along with his Guinness, and by half time an early numbness had set in. With three converted penalties apiece, the sides were level. Lou enjoyed rugby as much as the next baboon, but not under these conditions; his mob had arrived early enough to get seats, but when he got crushed up against a panelled wall, Lou abandoned hope and went outside to get some air. There was nowhere to sit there either, so leaving the roar of the second half behind him he broke one of his golden rules and entered a nearby burger joint, where he sat alone with a carton of chips. Deciding to stay for a while, he fished Feeney's masterpiece from his bag and took a quick decco. It seemed to start with some utter nonsense, an introduction comparing rugby to the great mythological cycles of Celtic prehistory. Whereas Ireland and Wales, and to a lesser extent Scotland, had a rich mythological base,

England had no native tradition. Beowulf and the other texts had come from the continent. As a result, England had colonised and pillaged other cultures for their myths.

Was the man bonkers? Had Lou crossed the Irish Sea to read *this*?

Feeney hadn't finished: because the English were great collectors and annotators, they'd given all they'd acquired abroad a clear structure, pedantic but highly organised, and this was reflected in the way they played rugby: the English side was always efficient and persistent in a well-drilled way, whereas the Celts were prone to disorder, like their myth cycles, relying on brilliant passages of swift movement and extemporised personal genius.

What? Lou laughed out loud, causing the staff to fall silent and stare at him bovinely before their corporate manners returned to them. He shuffled through the manuscript, took in some of the tone, then bagged it again and returned to the pub. The Welsh crowd was even drunker now, less than ten still able to talk and the rest gaga with drink after a ferocious drinking match against the locals. Wales had won the game in the dying seconds, apparently, though Lou cared nothing about that now; he just wanted to get out of there. Eventually they left the fallen and headed for Hotel Oblivion.

Next day they left Ireland, only a small group by now; no one knew what had happened to the others, no one cared much either. Someone was passing a bottle round, Bushmills Red, and they were catching up again. As they left harbour the country disappeared into mist, but that could have been the drink. Lou went up on deck and saw his mother's homeland ebb away from him; shrinking slowly, he became a boy again. His ma was tickling him and blowing in his ear and he was beginning to cry, he was shouting *stop ma or I'll wet meself* and she was doing raspberries in his ear; and then he felt sad and lonely and a bit sick, the Bushmills an oilslick on the strand of his tongue. When the girl with the red dragon hat came up on deck again for a fag he tried it on but she turned on him.

He moved away from her and stood at the rail, his ears absorbing the murmur of the sea, swash and spindrift spraying the ship's sides, and into his mind came a few words from 'The Seafarer'...

> *how I wandered for a wretched winter on the ice-cold sea, exiled, bereft of friends, harnessed in frost, showered in hail...*

He retched over the side and watched the girl waddle away in the shimmer of his own spew-tears. What a mess. *Heave.* What a hopeless shit he was. *Heave.*

He made paper planes with a dozen or so sheets from Dermot Feeney's famous book, watched them plunge down to the water; a few fluttered on deck. After a while he lost patience, tossed the rest over the rail and watched them scatter away, a flock of A4 seagulls. They made a pattern of shrouds on the water. Some of the sheets wrapped themselves around funnels and spars; he watched them dispassionately, waiting for them to slip away. Grasping the rails, he observed the cosmos of the sea again, and its faraway dots passing slowly from port to starboard, towards the horizon. Ships in the night. Noah a distant fleck, a mote in the eye of history. The Fir Bolg arriving, or maybe Tuatha De Danann. Saint Brendan the Navigator, on his seven-year voyage to the Isle of the Blessed with his cargo of fourteen pilgrims and three unbelievers. Over there, moving ever so slowly beneath a vast blue-grey dome. All dead now. Lou felt the memory stick through the fabric of his anorak and considered its fate. Over the side? But no, it was so pretty and mystical. A man's mind in a morsel. Great mind, nano technology. And as for Lou... nano mind, great technology?

It took forever to get home, it felt like years. For a while they sat in a pub on Holy Island, waiting for Holyhead to arrive in the new world, but that never looked likely so they caught a train and went to sleep. Lou woke up in Chester, caught another train back home. Some of them, apparently, went all the way to London, asleep like flamingoes with crooked necks, waking up with enormous, head-banging hangovers in Euston. Bloody chaos.

Catrin was surprisingly good about it. Just a touch of sarcasm when she opened the door.

Home is the hero, she said softly.

He observed the newly apparent swell of her belly and smiled a foolish, boyish smile.

Did that happen while I was away, he asked, for the bump seemed more obvious.

She kissed him on the cheek, almost mumsily, in the hallway, then ordered him upstairs for a shower. He woke the next morning on a large bean cushion in the new nursery, fresh paint trickling through his nostrils. He must have gone there after the shower, feeling emotional still. He lay on his side, looking at his handiwork, his commitment to biology. A big man in a baby's room. The tsunami of biology, a huge pheremonal wave crossing the universe. Each procreation was only a small piece of flotsam, really. What had he done? Lou noticed that his eyes were damp. His life was out of control and he was having a problem with scale again. Now he was inside the memory stick, in a small boat with a man, fishing. Long ago. And he wondered who that man was.

II

He was back in his room, the same old room, but the world around him had changed. The Irish trip had left a strange echo in his head, and the old simplicities had gone. He seemed to be two people now: the old Lou, whom he still mostly liked, and a new Lou, malevolent and cunning. He seemed to be morphing, and symptoms included an insecurity with scale and perspective. Was he a big man or a small man? One moment he seemed to be standing on the deck of a ferry in the Irish Sea, the next he was on the deck of a midget ferry crossing his computer screen.

And the sky had grown; it was huge, beyond human comprehension. The sky was the main arena now – a massive amphitheatre in which his own little life seemed utterly insignificant. Perhaps he'd spent too much time inside the micro-world of his computer, having fallen like everyone else into an eat-me, drink-me rabbit hole. Or perhaps it was Big M who was responsible, though he'd be an old man by now, if he was alive at all. He'd been such a *big* man, in every way. Physically big, mentally big, emotionally big. People had loved him, lots of people. And Lou? How many people had loved Lou? Not so many, really. His baby in Catrin's womb, would that baby love him most of all?

Back at his desk he felt a new sensation: his bee-hive cell at the college had changed into a dungeon. Stuck in there, sealed in his honeyless wax hexagon, would he be able to write a book about a hero, or would he take the easy route and destroy Feeney's masterpiece?

Lou logged on and waited for his bunch of daffs to appear.

He'd already put the Irish memory stick on his desk and he took it up now, cradled it in his left hand and lifted it right up to his eyes, so that he could study it closely, as a giant Gulliver might study a

Lilliputian or a Blefuscudian. In this light it looked like a tiny see-through mummy, embalmed in green plastic, with mechanical entrails and two blank little eyes where the stick connected to the computer. There was an intriguing double row of numbers on the flip side: they had to mean something to someone, he thought. Looking at the stick from the obverse side, its inner workings looked like a car park viewed from high above, with rows of identical, miniscule vehicles parked in neat silvery lines. Their virtual owners would be inside the stick somewhere, he thought, tinkering about with circuit testers and almost-invisible screwdrivers. Men in white coats and intelligent-looking scientific specs, as per the television adverts. Stock images. Clipboards and security swipe-cards. Doctorates from cyber universities.

Lou slipped the stick into one of the USB ports and opened it up. There were three folders, entitled M1, M2 and M3. A simple soul, Dermot Feeney. And stupid: his life's work had just entered a twilight zone of extreme vulnerability; with a few deft movements and double clicks, Lou could eradicate a whole brain's volume of knowledge. The thought of it. The sheer naked power of it.

Instead, he copied the files onto his desktop and left the originals in the memory stick. For now. Those little scientists would be running around inside, having a massive panic attack, someone shouting *who the feck did that* with a Galway accent. Claxons sounding, red lights flashing above doors. Then the all-clear. A smooth female voice, texture of melting chocolate. *Will the quantum version of Dr Dermot Feeney please go to USB port three. Everyone else can stand down now, the emergency is over. Our precious hives have been borrowed by a higher agency, a mouse-god going by the name of Llwyd McNamara, stealer of honey. Go back to your cars, take the day off. Better still, retire. Enjoy a picnic with your families in the sylvan groves which lie, reputedly, in the green memory sticks of your forefathers. Live life to the full. Throw down your notional, almost imperceptible tools. Workers of the cyber-world unite; you have nothing to lose but your micro-chains.*

In his head, Lou heard the soft scuff of many tiny soles on corridor floors as the internees fled.

He almost removed the stick to check it. Llwyd McNamara, he said to himself, you're losing the plot m'boy. Whilst imagining this cyber activity he fiddled about with Feeney's chapters, trying to find the best place for them on his screen; he settled, eventually, on the bottom right-hand corner. They looked like three fresh tombstones in a cyber cemetery; perhaps he ought to have a nice white wall around them and a slate-roofed lychgate. A line of black cars, and a chrysanthemum wreath spelling out the name Dermot. Would that be possible? He could always ask IT, make a joke of it.

A fly landed on the screen, on a daffodil trumpet, and squatted motionlessly on the picture. He wafted it away, but it bothered him now, so he followed it around the room. Lou McNamara, small game hunter. Why didn't he leave it alone? In no time at all it'd be gone through a window but no, Lou couldn't stop himself. Picking up a magazine on the way, he splatted it on the main window, smearing it in an impasto paste on the glass; its viscera reminding him of the memory stick's innards. Then he reproached himself for inflicting death on a hapless animal much smaller than himself; a pall of self-disgust clasped his head and pushed him down into his chair. He thought of his little baby in Catrin's womb and made many imprecations, beseeching all powers above and below for a safe passage through this world and the next for himself and his progeny. Closing his eyes, he channelled his thoughts towards the Blakean gods up there in the soft white cirrus clouds between his brain and the bone cupola of his skull, gods with flowing locks who looked down on man from the softly illuminated skies of the dura mater. He begged them to ignore the assassination of the fly and to spare his baby in any similar scenario which might occur in future days, whensoever and whenas his dear wee babbie might be threatened by a huge magazine-wielding psychopath, simian or otherwise. There were no gods there really, thought Lou, but it was just as well to play safe. As he'd noted in his academic paper, all the gods in his head seemed to be elderly, downward-looking gentlemen with lots of nice wavy hair plus the muscle tone of those sunburnt bikers with white horseshoe moustaches, all well past seventy, who were minded to live for ever on the trailer parks of Miami. And then there was the Greek scenario, with a posse of unpredictable gods milling around in the human world like a gang of moody teenagers indulging in a spot of cider 'n pills mayhem down at the local park. Was there a heaven or a hell? One of his colleagues had remarked that the only likely difference between the two was that one had wi-fi and the other didn't.

Down to business. Opening the first file, M1, he scrolled through it at speed to get the gist of things. Much of it he knew in outline, but some of the details were fascinating.

Big M, or *Your Man* to the Irish and *Little Manny* to the English, tilting at irony, had been the second-best rugby player of his generation in the world. The best, by a thin patina of cold mud, had been his brother, Ben. They'd played together in the Welsh side during the glory years, a monstrous, mythical side which was never beaten, breaking record after record. Unusually large for a hooker, brother Ben had captained the side and led by example from the front. Ferociously fit and strong, he had a good head on him too, and his brilliant tacticianship had inspired quaking fear in every side they'd played against. His public nickname was *the bridge*, because his team mates frequently walked right over him, quite literally, during their rolling mauls, leaving him spread-eagled in the mud. His private pet name was *the blind mouse* because the little rodent tattooed in blue on his chest had no eyes; he'd left the tattoo parlour in a hurry, for reasons unknown, though he was a lusty man and it could have been a passing girl who'd caught his fancy. Feeney also asserted that Ben's mouse was the origin of the phrase *playing a blinder.*

His brother, Big M, was in the second row, right behind him, a fearsome lock who rolled the opposition as easily as an elephant rolls tree trunks. They'd had a telepathic understanding, expanding the maul into a match-winning gambit which had proved unstoppable. They were very strong, very determined, and very quick.

All this Lou knew, but it was Feeney's painstaking research which provided the chapter's highlights. For instance, Lou hadn't known that Big M commanded a big cult following over the water, where he was regarded as something of an icon. Feeney had uncovered a number of pub shrines in various corners of Ireland, featuring pictures and scarves and match programmes arranged into corner or window altars; at least seven pubs had been renamed in his honour. Feeney had been to these places, talked to the locals, taken pictures. He may have genuflected at those shrines himself, thought Lou, such was the awe in the writer's approach to Big M. There was a considerable trade in memorabilia on eBay, though prices were kept relatively low because Big M had been a great giver of gifts, and there was plenty of stuff out there.

Feeney had also uncovered another amazing fact. All the men who'd played for Wales had a small blue mouse tattooed on their chests, on the left pec, rather like the translators of ancient Carthage who reputedly had a parrot tattooed in the same place.

The mouse was a secret among the Welsh players, apparently – the mark of their fraternity. It transpired that the famous rugby coach and commentator Gaerwyn James, writing in the *Western Mail*, had once compared a particularly chaotic Welsh scrum to a family of desperate mice fighting over the world's last piece of cheese. This had become a bit of a running joke among the players, and eventually – in a drunken extravagance after a big win – the entire side had a mouse tattooed on their chests. Dr Feeney indicated that this was still going on, and he had a picture (of a bathful of coal-faced men) which would prove it.

Lou returned to the Ireland frozen in his memory and savoured the smells of those country bars once again; the vestigial odours of bacon and cabbage, cow-breath and rolled-down wellies, whiskey and porter, gum-clenched ciggies, butter and bullshit, marigolds and manyana, musky vestments, uilleann leather, the very aftertang of the island's epic history. Other than the ancient on-off relationship between the two countries, there was nothing to explain this reverence for Big M over the water. He'd obviously struck a chord there. Feeney had uncovered another fact, that Big M had been a great lover and player of Irish music, taking his fiddle with him whenever he went over for an international. Some of his favourite tunes were listed: the jigs – *Apples in Winter, The Barefoot Boy, The Cat in the Corner, Crabs in the Skillet, The Geese in the Bog, The Hag with the Money, Walk out of it, Hogan*. And the reels – *Don't Bother Me, Fair and Forty, The New Potatoes, Paddy Ryan's Dream, The Tent at the Fair*. He'd played the O'Carolan planxties fit to make you weep, and he had his own hornpipe, *Big M in the Barn with Maureen*.

There was a picture of him, with a fiddle tucked under his film-star jaw, standing in the middle of a céilidh, all eyes upon him, his bow blurred on the strings, an early snowfall of rosin on the upper bout. Passion in his eyes. Voluminous check shirt and baggy corduroy trousers over a pair of fancy leather boots, Cuban heeled and very expensive. Archetypal rugby forward, archetypal warrior. Was he playing that fiddle or sharpening it for battle?

Feeney had the gall to go off on a riff about perspective; how Big M had introduced a new spatial awareness to rugby, in the way Giotto had introduced depth to medieval art; gifted with rare insight, they'd both construed a new vision, the third dimension, one on canvas, the other on grass... Feeney introduced the word *supersight.*

Lou laughed out loud again, and read on. It would be a pleasure to destroy this stuff. Hogwash and bumfluff. Feeney's mind had gone before his body.

The story switched to the famous match at Ireland's old ground, Lansdowne Road. The Irish Tragedy, as it became known, happened at the end of a famous home international series which had seen the best Irish side for many years. Wales and Ireland had won all their games in the run-up, and the crunch match was played in front of a capacity crowd on a fine day in early March. Ireland was hotly tipped to upset the applecart and depose the Welsh as champions. The bookies had gone with Ireland, and a record TV audience saw both sides adopt highly aggressive tactics in the first half, hoping to establish physical superiority. The second half resembled the final tourney on the opening day at Vespasian's colosseum – a fight to the death; hand-to-hand combat, gallons of blood. There was hardly a man without an injury of some sort, and the crowd was stunned into silence.

Eventually, holding a slender three-point lead, which had come from a penalty, the Welsh were forced to defend from a perilous position – a scrum right in front of their own posts. Two minutes to go, Irish put-in. As the ball went in, the Welsh managed a tremendous push which forced the Irish to wheel back in disarray. The ensuing melee lasted for ages, and when the ball eventually emerged from the black hole of the scrum a huge roar went up because the oval grail had ended up in the spade-like hands of Your Man, hero of all Wales and sometime hero of Ireland too, Big M. He careered down the pitch, shrugging off tackles like an oak-built cyborg; when he reached the Irish try line he fell rather than dived over it, only half-conscious by then. It seemed like a tremendous victory, but as the players slowly unpeeled themselves from the ground, ready for the conversion attempt, it became apparent that Big M's brother, Ben the hooker, had been very badly hurt in the initial scrum. Worse, he'd been mortally injured – his neck had been broken. An awful silence descended on Lansdowne Road; the crowd was turned to stone, a mass of pillars wedged together like the basalt columns of the Giant's Causeway. But nothing could be done; Ben died on the pitch, surrounded by his team mates. The Welsh had won, but at a terrible price. Stunned, the crowd melted away. Lou had seen the old newspaper reports, yellow and sad; page after page showing the players grouped around their supine captain, and the first-aid team bent over him, their stretcher laid out ready to take his body away. There was a famous *Daily Mirror* edition, the whole of the front page taken up with a black-edged picture of Big M, lying there on the churned-up pitch, all grainy and heroic. The event became embalmed in mythology, in the same vein as the famous Scarlets victory over the All Blacks; if everyone who claimed to be there on that fateful day had actually been there, the entire population of

Western Europe would have been present. Famous writers rearranged history so that they could remember seeing the Morrigan standing at the ford, washing the hero's garments and foretelling death; poets recalled signs and auguries, the unearthly blood-call of carrion crows from the grandstand roof as the match began, rivers of rusty red coursing down the corrugated gutters.

This, then, was the event which became known as the Irish Tragedy.

Much had been written about it, so Lou knew the story intimately. Only seven of the original team had been able to leave for home the next day, the rest hospitalised. Then, upon arriving on Holy Island, they'd embarked on an epic bender which lasted for longer than any other bender in history; indeed, some claimed it was still going on, which explained the number of pubs in Holyhead and the superstar boozers who propped up the bars of the town. Big M had played a series of laments on his fiddle, and this – according to Feeney – was the original cause of the town's lugubrious and unhappy appearance, a state which had lasted to this very day. At that time a string broke when he was beginning the *caoineadh os cionn coirp* – the lament for the dead in Ireland, but he carried on playing to the end and no one even noticed.

The coda was sadder than anything which preceded it; in a twist worthy of a Jacobean tragedy, or a prime-time TV soap, a sister to Ben and Big M, the fêted beauty Branwen, was found wandering on the western shores of Anglesey in a distressed state. The next day's headlines touted psychiatric problems caused by domestic abuse, even a cocaine habit and alcoholism, but at the subsequent inquest many of her friends attested to her sanity, and drug/alcohol tests were negative. After that it was natural for the papers to wring every drop they could from the tragedy. *She died of a broken heart*, screamed a *Daily Post* headline. Her simple grave in the dunes at Aberffraw soon became a shrine, permanently decked with flowers and messages from fans – probably the same people who left flowers and totems around Phil Lynott's grave at St Fintan's in Dublin, thought Lou. Cynical Lou, who closed the file and guided it to the recycle bin. But before he killed it off he had second thoughts, and left the file in limbo. Perhaps it might come in useful for his own research. So he left it there. He could always restore it; bring it back from the dead if he wanted to. A sort of virtual Easter. A miniature Oberammergau on his screen. The thought intrigued him; he could see himself in the crowd.

However, sitting around in his room would butter no parsnips. He had to get out there among the plebs, hear their stories, take their testimonies. That's the way history had gone, down the vermicular holes of the hoi polloi. Once upon a time the world's annals had recorded the acts of supreme beings as they lounged about in their summer playgrounds, feasting on warm cascades of ambrosia; but now history was all about the smashed-up playgrounds of the worthless, atomised humans around him. Once, history had been a matter of fate and fertility in groves and palaces; now it was about foolishness and dysfunction on derelict council estates. The action had moved from the asphodel fields of Elysium to the cracked concrete meadows of modern urbanism, a bankrupt society living in ruined readymix glebes. Lou hated it. He avoided public transport, he didn't want to touch the great unwashed. What was the point of their story? His hand moused the cursor to the bin, and left it there, poised over the *empty recycle bin* icon. But once again he stayed his hand and let it be. Revenge would come later and it would come on a colder day than this, thought Lou. The thought of it made him sexually excited and he phoned Catrin for a chat, hoping to warm things up for later. He'd discovered that this peculiar quest of his, for a formless and generic revenge on Feeney, had the same effect on him as watching porn on his computer. He'd have to google the subject; in the meantime, he was quite happy to sit back and enjoy the experience.

Then his mind echoed again, and he remembered a name from the folder in the bin. Hotel Corvo. Could it be the same place? If it was, what a hell of a coincidence.

He retraced his steps to the bin, restored the file, and scrolled to the end of Feeney's first chapter. Yes, there it was, Hotel Corvo, on the cliffs of West Wales. Well fancy that. He knew it intimately. He read to the end of the chapter intently, and as he did so a series of pictures flashed through his mind, from the past.

After that bender to end all benders on Holy Island, Big M had decided to hang up his rugby boots once and for all, but since he had no plans in mind, his team mate Pryderi made him an offer which went something like this:

Big M me ole pal, you've been a good friend to me these many years. I came into the side a pup, wet behind the ears, but you looked after me and now it's payback time. I'm going back to the wife, I'm packing up this mad maul of a life, I'm going back to where I belong, to the high cliffs of West Wales. Hotel Corvo, and my lovely jubbly wifey. Coming, mate? We could have a fine old time running the joint together. Seven bars and a hundred rooms, plenty of fun to be had;

you can run the bars and I'll run the hotel side with the missus. And there's me ole mum, Rhiannon, she could do with a bit of company, know what I mean? So how about it me sweet palaroony, get yer dancin' shoes, let's head out to the place where I love best, let's watch the sun go down on an empty sea, let's smoke some decent hash, play some music, chill...

Lou logged off and shut down his computer. For a while he sat at his desk, with his head in his hands, fingering a suspiciously hairless patch on his crown, and looking at his fruit bowl. A single banana was beginning to turn brown and it needed eating, but he liked them green and firm.

Hotel Corvo. He'd been there in his youth. A long time ago. His memory held a clear picture of a big white building on a promontory, black-painted doors and windows, crenelated rooftops. Big rookery, a raucous cacophany in the evenings. Throb of the sea below. Great storms, shipwrecks, and colonies of noisy seals. Flotsam and jetsam, plenty of places to explore. No land in sight, a crow's nest view of the ocean. All the way from left to right, a vast body of water without islands or rocks. Mesolithic people living in a nearby hunting camp must have seen the exact same vista, without change. You could show them a snapshot and maybe they'd grin, point towards home. Or maybe they'd react like those aboriginees of urban myth who'd looked at the white man's television and failed to see anything happening on the screen.

Beyond the horizon Ireland, and then nothing at all. Hotel Corvo loomed large and squat on the headland, dreamt about for years by an eccentric and then built as a castle, like so many seaside hotels from the beginning of the twentieth century. It would cost a fortune to build now, but in those days labour was cheap. Lou remembered a fortress of a building, servants in livery, maids in black dresses with white linen aprons and mop caps. There was a huge fire-place in the main hall, everything shone. Secluded alcoves, huge red sofas, newspapers and magazines from the *Country Life* sector. But there were bars down below for the locals too, and these had been very popular because they were far enough away from home: ideal for shenanigans, illicit meetings and male pursuits.

Old sea salts, tenor farmers stoked up on whiskey, posh retirees from the armed forces, young men having a lark, they were all there. Mostly men in those days, though Saturday night dances flushed out some of the local girls.

So Big M said yes to Pryderi. *Let's have some fun.* Posh little cocktail bar for the smart set and a lounge bar for the country set upstairs; a private bar for clubs and societies; a spit 'n sawdust bar for the workers, a nightclub, a restaurant, and a nice little personal bar for Big M himself, hidden away in a cubby hole off the servants' staircase...

So that's what they did, off they went to Hotel Corvo, and they celebrated their new pact. Big dinner, posh nosh for family and friends. Pryderi sat next to his wife Ziggy, and Big M, in his best bib and tucker, sat next to Rhiannon, a nice mature lady but still pretty gorgeous. She and Big M hit it off immediately. *Phew!* said Pryderi, *this is going like a dream.*

Between courses, Rhiannon and Big M chatted, glanced at each other, joked a little. Both of them had some grieving to do. Sitting on clifftops in the sun, on pink slopes of thrift, letting time pass by.

She asked him what he planned.

He'd walk around on the shore, thinking. That was his plan. He would sit by the newly flowered gorse watching little green shield bugs drying out in the sunshine. Look at gannets plunging their yellow spears into the waves. Go swimming, watch the anemones going all shy when the tide turned. Feel the sand between his toes. Go crabbing, surfing, all the things he did as a kid. Let some time slip by, arrange headstones for his brother and sister, beautifully carved words on plain Welsh slate.

And her?

Something similar. Walk along the coastal path. Come to terms with the past. Watch the felucca clouds go by, since they were pilgrims too. Build up trade at the hotel, make enough money in summer to go travelling all winter. Have a nice easy life. No complications, she wanted no complications. None.

And there would always be horses in her life; she rode every day if she could.

The meal went on for a long time, but that was OK. They felt relaxed together, and they got slowly drunk in each other's company. Later, outside on the balcony, watching the moon on the sea, she leant on him, put her back against his chest and rested her chin on her wine glass. He felt good, firm but soft too. She liked his shoes, they looked expensive and well-made. Light tan leather, only four eyelets. Classy.

Spring was such a good time to be alive, said Big M, he loved it when the land was covered in that sensuous white mist, when the earth began to warm up. Special time of the year, buds and leaves popping out everywhere and birds dashing about. Nature busy. And later, a sleepy heat haze blanking out the sea. Lovely. People didn't matter then, they disappeared. Just nature surfing the big wave of spring.

They didn't bother kissing, neither felt the need. They slept together child-naked on fresh sheets that first night, their skins slightly flushed with a suggestion of early desire. All night they faced each other on their sides, hands linked together below their chins as if sharing a bedtime prayer, just looking at each other when they woke, like a couple of kids in love. Didn't need to talk much. Nice when that happens. When you can't remember going to sleep and you wake up feeling entirely different. Refreshed. Knowing that everything's about to change.

Big M could hear their bodies talking to each other, biology's soft bubble below the surface. Primal desire. The tingle of new skins meeting.

Can you hear it? he asked Rhiannon. A man of the sea, he described faraway whales calling to each other in the deeps, dolphin schools sending messages in hydro-morse.

And what could she hear?

A muffled confederacy of horses together below a canopy of trees, three fields away. Icterines and passerines on the wing above, coming in on the spring air. Swifts, swallows and martins. Old world warblers and flycatchers, the skylarks. She could hear them above.

These were the mysterious moments of lovers in

the night. Secret, cabbalistic. They were the last generation, said Rhiannon, who listened to nature. The last to describe the world without man's constant presence; to describe it as watchers, not as controllers. The last to know the song of the willow warbler and the chiff-chaff.

They could sense the long line of cliffs going away from them, along the coast; and stretching far behind them they could sense a small kingdom of rich green countryside. They were living in a natural paradise. They would go for car rides together to explore the country, enjoy the sights. They would watch bees and butterflies combing the mayflower blossom; they would see wood mice sunning themselves on country walls. They would see adders dancing and lambs prancing.

They would see it all.

III

Lou was in bed with Catrin, lying with his head parked lightly on her bubble. He was intrigued by the hidden scene inside her; their little bald actor, with his cummerbund placenta, alone in his dressing room, waiting patiently for the five-minute call. It was just amazing the way you could effect a rough docking, like a couple of play-doh spaceships hitting turbulence, and nine months later you'd have another version of the eternal drama, ready to appear in a slightly different provincial theatre. Lou was excited and intrigued by the activities within. Pregnancy had been good for them both. Catrin looked wonderful and Lou *was going to be a good father* – he'd said it and he meant it. Then his rampant hormones got the better of him for a second time that morning;

fortunately, Catrin was just as horny herself. When they were at it, in medias res, he thought of the girl in the dragon hat on the ferry and momentarily lost his rhythm. What a shit he was. Later, after a breakfast of toast and marmalade – they'd run out of milk for cereal, thanks to Catrin's urges – he went to the shops for some emergency supplies, then set off for West Wales and the reunion with himself at Hotel Corvo. A foreign-sounding female voice had laughed lightly at the other end of the line when he'd phoned to book.

Plenty of roomz zir, yez vi haff plenty ov roomz right now.

Perhaps he should have stayed in the village and snuck up to the hotel at night, as he'd done as a teenager, but he couldn't be bothered. When he entered the coastal belt a thick white mist was rolling in off the sea and cars were driving on full headlights. He switched on his rear fog lamp and wondered why it gave him such childish pleasure to do so; it was something one did so rarely in life, and there was a slight sense of virtuousness and righteousness, of reacting nobly in a challenging situation. The road wasn't quite as he remembered it and the journey took longer than he'd anticipated, so evening was drawing on by the time he arrived. Hotel Corvo was smaller than he remembered, of course, and much the worse for wear. Despite this, he wasn't disappointed. He'd looked forward to coming back, though he knew the dangers of expectation, and as a precaution he'd deliberately dampened his hopes in advance. So it was nice to take his blue BMW through the curves of the driveway, and to enjoy the tilts and timbres of the narrow road leading up to the hilltop. The rooks or jackdaws were cawing their way towards bed as he closed the lid of the boot and made his way to reception. It didn't take him long to establish that the hotel was an empty and decaying ghost ship ploughing her way through heavy seas; at the edge of the world now, ready to topple over.

He'd arranged for a member of staff to take him straight to the village and off they went as soon as he'd dumped his hold-all in his room. Down in the white-shrouded bay he skirted the rocks and went out to the tideline, so that he could savour the salty air again and let the scene stir his memory. The mist enveloped him and he felt cool and distant and isolated. He listened for foghorns, but his invisible world was completely silent as droplets of vapour began clinging to his pullover and hair. A bell clanged distantly, and a heron shrieked from the direction of the marshes.

He'd been sixteen when they came here, Lou and his freckly ma. While she worked as a barmaid at Hotel Corvo he'd spent the summer making friends, discovering sex and dope and cheap booze, surfing and spending all night in the woods with other kids, exploring each other around campfires, popping some pills and getting dizzy. Then they'd left, as suddenly as they came, when the season ended. His ma had been quiet, depressed, perplexed. She never was the same again – she put on a lot of weight and didn't bother with her looks any more. Something happened to her that summer at Hotel Corvo.

Lou walked up through the village, which was

much the same as it was in his youth. More holiday homes perhaps, they looked tidier and better cared for than the rest. The shop and post office had shut, as per normal, and one of the chapels had closed, new dormer windows giving it a fresh view of the holy kingdom.

Up he went, slowly, looking out for landmarks; the hollow tree where he'd hidden his swimming gear and bottles (tree still there, but no bottles) and a slat in a slate fence onto which he'd carved a girl's name; Ros Smedley, his second great passion that year (the name was still there, but the slender girl he remembered had been swallowed by the void, probably married with kids now, leaving a strange longing inside Lou). His first summer of love came back to him as steadily as the waves crashing in the mist below. Hard goosepimples on experimental young skin, fumbled flesh, electricity fizzing through his fingers as the AA bra or bikini top eventually came undone. Week-long snogs. Volcanic brain movements and a near-constant hard-on. Wonderful, amazing days. And every evening, his skin still tingling, his hair damp and his feet slopping about in a pair of pumps which he was meant to grow into, he'd stalk uphill towards Hotel Corvo, to mingle among the men in the public bar, pretending to be one of their sons. After the initial gambit came off he became a regular, though the bar staff knew well enough he wasn't eighteen, turning a blind eye because they knew his ma worked upstairs. It was a time when pubs were at their most popular, operating at full capacity. They were still a way of life for most people, places where they went to be social, to look for sex and to find work. They'd been the country's social centres since the chapels and churches emptied. The men played the old games, darts and dominoes, and there would always be one who'd start to sing in a wayward tenor voice towards the end of the night. Men still whistled then. Girls would sit tentatively with girly drinks, their cashmere pullovers draped over their shoulders and smudges of lipstick on their glasses. Drinks had nicknames like *snakebite* or *leg-opener*. Even in the daytime the place would be bustling with men in transit between jobs, or taking a break from home duties, or drinking their holidays away. There was always a healthy interaction between the generations, not like today's scene with a bored barmaid reading a magazine, a few oldies ignored in the corner and a big open space, then some kids being moody with a cheap bottle of vodka hidden away in a bag. Lou called them the *Friends* generation because they just wanted to be in their own little TV sitcom modelled on the American product; it was what they aspired to – cool banter in a cool place, a bunch of schmucks livin' the dream. The camera was always on them.

He approached the hotel with a frisson travelling through him, and he dropped his shoulders like a cat-burglar as the hulk of the building began to loom overhead. A row of lights, coming from the downstairs bar, lured him onwards. The place was much quieter now; there was no hubbub coming from inside, no cars coming and going. He peered into the long window which fronted the building and saw nothing at first, just a sea of empty tables and chairs; but when his eyes reached the long mahogany bar, over against the far wall, his eyes registered a series of silhouettes leaning against the woodwork. Amazingly, he recognised them all from the rear, by their shapes. Like seven old mythological beings or Easter Island statues carved in stone, they were still there: each outline stepping up or down against the yellow burr of the bar lights, a mountain range of dark blue hills set against the late evening light. He knew them all by their stance and their body talk; a lifetime's mannerisms had been condensed into a slouch here or a stoop there. They were the survivors; everyone else in that bar had disappeared into the mist outside, or into the mists of time, but these last stragglers had defied statistics and probability; they'd survived the many winters which separated them all from Lou. The rest had gone. None of those hulks should have been there; they'd smoked and drank and caroused and misbehaved enough for a thousand men, but they'd got away with it. Strange, how it worked out, thought Lou. You never knew who'd last the years, but you always had a suspicion. The human life force seemed to have an atomic quality to it, discernible in passing bodies; a sort of quantum tweeting by the pheremones.

Lou crept stealthily towards the bar, hoping to surprise them, but he should have known better; what those men had, more than anything else, was a supersensitive perception of their environment. One of them, he remembered, could chat to you engagingly while simultaneously listening to many other conversations going on around him, as if he were a listening device. It was quite unbelievable what he could pick up. As a result he was a walking encylopaedia of local gossip, going back to the birth of the village; indeed, through hearsay and rumour he could return, vicariously, to the dawn of local history. At the same time as his ears swivelled to and fro his clever, knowing eyes were scanning the scene for any additional material which might reinforce his aural intake. He was a plasterer by trade, doing just enough work every morning to fund his drinking for the rest of the day; and since he'd worked in almost every house in the vicinity during his lifetime, he could localise all the information coming his way, room by room. Add to this a formidable memory, and what you had was a data bank matching the national archive at Kew.

They'd had sex lives to match the rich and famous; if the OS maps had carried symbols for their mating spots instead of castles and churches the landscape would be cluttered with their insignias. It wasn't that they were crude bucolic casanovas; for a start, they'd lived for a long time and had known lots of women. It was more than that: they had charm, yes natural homegrown charm. A bit threadbare now, perhaps, but still discernible in the way they gave you their sincere and undivided attention when you were with them – a perfectly natural form of flattery. And here they were, like a coven of old spiders, huddled up in a corner trying to avoid the painter's brush, hiding from the fresh paint of time and change. That wasn't mist he could see through the window, thought Lou, it was a glistening band of silky strands stretching out towards every bedroom in the vicinity, because they'd all wandered away from their own webs many times; they were loopy oversexed spiders who didn't know the confines of the average cobweb.

So they greeted him now, softly, bought him a drink and made a fuss of him in their old-fashioned way, because they knew exactly who Llwyd McNamara was from the moment they saw a BMW climbing the foggy hill to Hotel Corvo.

Maureen's son, isn't it? said one of them in his sea-cave voice, but he wasn't asking, he knew. Western shores bred such men all over the world. Shy, diffident and subdued, but self-sufficient and resourceful. Gifted in unexpected ways and full of small wonders, like the rockpools below. Quick-witted and droll, but essentially sad. After all, the sea itself was basically sad. Small sun-burnt faces framed in the windows of departing cars at the end of fine summer days had something to do with it, perhaps. Or maybe it was the sea's parental moods – they made you wary after a while. Shorelines had a liminal sadness about them because you'd look at a group of kids playing on the sand and you'd be there yourself immediately, the beach was such a communal experience, but one of those kids was always you and you'd see how time passed, you'd see right into the mechanism of time, it was like looking into a watch and seeing a tiny version of yourself walking along the rim of a cog; you'd feel sad, and your own tristesse would be added to a communal melancholia which festered in the creeks and pools and lodged in barnacle clumps on the rocks all around you. You'd see yourself being eroded in step with the cliffs and the bays; here at the edge of the world you saw yourself slipping away. The shore was a playground for children but it was a graveyard for memories. Life always ended with your own Titanic going down near the shore – but instead of the orchestra playing you'd hear your own memories scratching away at the porthole windows.

Those shipwrecked men in the bar at Hotel Corvo, they all remembered Maureen the freckled Irish girl for various reasons, but there was one communal memory which they wouldn't share with her son, on compassionate grounds. Once, Maureen had got drunk at the bar, after a shift, and something had happened. An embarrassing episode, followed by a scene. These men had seen it all, witnessed

Maureen being exposed and compromised. The male involved – Leda to her swan – had been the manager of the bars, Big M himself, who knew they were being watched. It wasn't that he was an exhibitionist, it was just that he didn't care. Women couldn't and didn't try to resist him; sex was part of his daily diet, like food and drink. Everyone knew that, even his regular girl, Rhiannon.

Morality seemed to fall asleep whenever he opened his flies. He joked about it, and nobody seemed to mind. He'd pour himself a drink, raise his glass, pose ridiculously with his chest out, and say *I'm a Sex God you know*. He could say it in a way which was cheesy and funny and a bit sad too, but never really offensive, and in not trying to get away with it he got away with it. Big M was a sex god. In the misty, numinous world of Hotel Corvo, nobody cared. His libido came and went with the tide. After a while, they didn't even notice it.

Lou leant against the bar, by now an eighth silhouette in the mountain range. He felt at home with these men, despite all the differences. He suspected that they knew something he didn't – he'd picked that up when he was a kid. It was partly the reason for being here. They shared rounds and he started to feel drunk, because he hadn't had any food. No one else came in – this bar at the end of the universe was just for them, it seemed.

'So what happened to Big M, the rugby hero who ran the bars?' asked Lou while he was quizzing them about all the old faces.

'He just disappeared,' said the man by his side. None of them was particularly forthcoming, since they were all re-running their clips of Maureen, tearstained under her tousled red hair.

So Lou made his excuses and sidled off to the restaurant to get some food inside him before he got sloshed. He was the only one in there, and when the food arrived he realised why. Still, it filled a hole. He felt morose by now, sad that this place was on its last legs, like so many of Britain's pubs and hotels. The breathalyser had started the decline, and greedy middle men had syphoned off more and more, so that drinking out had become an expensive hobby.

Then television came to hypnotise the populace, and the computer screen, so that in no time at all the British were a nation of post-modernist zombies living a virtual life, most of it set in America. The roads were deserted, the land was empty. If you walked along a street at dusk before they closed their curtains you'd see them all sitting there, fettered to their bargain sofas, mesmerised by mediocrity. How supine they'd all become, thought Lou, they were just a bunch of pets with their paws in the air, waiting for their cable-powered masters to feed them a morsel or stroke their tums. How sad, how tragic that these places were empty – the robust universities of the poor, closed down and boarded up. All that humour and badinage gone, atomised into vapour inside a time capsule.

Knowing that he'd only delayed drunkenness, Lou returned to the bar and rejoined the shadows leaning against it. Although they must have downed another couple of rounds they were none the worse for it. Maybe that's why they'd survived for so long, thought Lou, they'd all paced themselves, and the pace had been fast all along. Life had been a marathon drinking session, interspersed with a few hours' work here or there to finance it.

One of them, a carpenter who made a fortune by painting distressed repro seascapes and selling them to the gullible, sat down at a nearby table to take the weight off his legs. Lou joined him in the roseate gloom, and they sat together comfortably on a settle running along a wall, with their backs to the faded crimson upholstery – Lou recognised its distinctive smell, beery and dusty. Drunk by now and chasing a double whiskey, he quizzed the carpenter about the consumptive decline of Hotel Corvo. He wanted to know why his ma had come here, but he was sensible enough to scout around the issue. The carpenter was happy to tell him the background story as he knew it.

Going back a generation, the hotel had fallen on hard times when the entrepreneur who'd built it died. Then a local lad, Pryderi, had bought it. No one knew how he'd got the money together, but everyone assumed that the spondoolicks had come from his burgeoning rugby career. He went on to play for Wales, said the carpenter, and he pointed to a row of photographs on the far wall, as if Lou didn't know about them already. Pryderi became the main man in the region, a bit of a lad and a general wheeler-dealer. Fancied himself. Girls, fast cars, friends on the council, dodgy deals. After he'd come back from Ireland with his team mate Big M, things really took off at the hotel. They built it up and, helped along by their good looks, charm, and legendary reputations, they turned the place into a goldmine.

But enough wasn't enough for Pryderi, said the carpenter. His wife Ziggy had been an ambitious little missy, cunning and devious. One of those clever little working-class girls who'd erased their accents and made the most of their abilities; they dressed well in an understated way, and found a guy who could make money. Pryderi was ideal: she'd pointed him in the right direction and urged him on. But somewhere along the line they'd over-extended, got into financial bother. And instead of going through the usual channels, Pryderi had gone underground for money. There had been regular trips across the border: first to Kent, then to Oxford. Every time he came back he was different; his moods became blacker, his silences longer. He'd sit at a table outside, looking at the sea, and he'd drink himself into a stupour.

Loan sharks? asked Lou.

Maybe, said the carpenter. But a carful of men had descended on Hotel Corvo one afternoon, quiet men in expensive suits, dark and sleek, and they'd had Irish accents. Coincidence maybe, but from that day onwards the silhouettes at the bar had never discussed the issue again in public, because they'd all thought of the same outfit when they saw those men – the IRA.

You sure about that? asked Lou.

No, just a hunch said the carpenter. What else would they be? The way they stood close together at the end of the bar drinking tonic water, their leader a wall-eyed man who surveyed you with his one good eye in a way which made you look away immediately. They'd stayed all day, eating and talking sparsely at a table outside, all of them with their backs to the gable end. He remembered the glare of the linen tablecloth and their crisp white shirts, done up to the top button but tieless; gold cufflinks, and bespoke alligator shoes from Carreducker. Smart as hell, and each of them with a wad of fifty quid notes rolled up in the back trouser pocket, as if they were at a gypsy funeral. No one except them was allowed to pay for drinks; they fed the bar for a whole afternoon, until they left shortly after nightfall. Maureen had brought out a lantern and they'd sat there smoking and talking quietly to Pryderi and Big M.

So Big M was in on all this, said Lou.

No, said the carpenter, Big M wanted nothing to do with it. Big M was a steady, regular guy. He'd had enough trouble in his life. Big M wanted a nice easy time running the bars, enjoying a few scoops with his friends at night, wandering around the county with his girl Rhiannon and generally living the good life.

What sort of man was he? asked Lou.

Really nice bloke, said the carpenter. Sound as a pound, easy going and fun to be with. No nasty bits at all, sunny side up all the time, great sense of humour. Incredibly quick on the uptake and good at everything he did. The carpenter recalled a wet Sunday afternoon when Big M had picked up a set of darts, and within a few hours he was beating all-comers. Same on the pool table, and the same when it came to drinking, he was good for a long enjoyable session. When he wanted to be alone he'd go off fishing, he'd take his big silver sea rod and he'd come back in a few hours with a bagful of bass, or the first mackerel of the season. Have a look for yourself, said the carpenter, pointing to the framed photographs on the wall.

And although he'd stared at them many times, Lou went over to look at them again.

There he was, Big M, at the centre of most of them; in the national rugby team, or behind the bar, or holding up a huge bass with a small crowd around him. Going up close, so that his nose almost touched the glass, he took a good look at the man. He was big, and still in good shape; broad-chested with a trace of a six pack underneath the t-shirt. Underneath the thin cotton Lou could make out the outline of a little blue mouse. The famous tattoo. Big M was clean shaven but dark chinned, an A-list magazine model if ever you saw one. There was something about the eyes which reminded him of someone, but he couldn't think who it was. There was a stand-out feature in all the pictures at Hotel Corvo: Big M always had a smart pair of shoes on his feet. Yes, Big M was a real dandy when it came to footwear, ranging from huge cowboy boots to brothel creepers, Oxfords, Bluchers, Chelsea boots and brogues, right down to daps and espadrilles, the man was a maniac for footwear. Lou was known for being natty down under himself, but he wasn't a fetishist. The carpenter made a joke of it.

Notice his feet? he said. *Always the smart shoes, but he crept around at night like a big cat, nothing on his feet at all, know what I mean?*

He grinned slyly and looked down at Lou's expensive trainers. He didn't say anything, but he couldn't help looking up towards the pictures again.

Lou ordered a last round of drinks before he went

to bed, and although they made a show of protesting, he insisted. *One last one, to remember the good old days*, he slurred. He was nowhere near as competent as this lot. He ordered a double Jameson, and watched the barman take the dust off the bottle before decanting the whiskey.

'Hasn't seen any action for a while,' said Lou when the bottle went back on the shelf.

'Not since Big M left, probably,' replied the barman. 'It was his favourite.'

They all raised their glasses and they toasted the good old days. It was a strange end to the evening, with Lou slumped on the settee and seven performing elephants swivelling in unison before raising their trunks to him; that's how it seemed to him. The whiskey was burning his pipes by now and he was feeling a bit sick.

'Pity to see the place like this,' he said thickly to no one in particular.

'Want to know why it's like this?' asked the carpenter, his head suddenly right next to his, large and pendulous.

'Sure,' said Lou.

'Then come with me,' said the carpenter, putting one hand lightly on his shoulder and pointing the other towards the door.

Lou stumbled after him, a shambolic figure by now. He must have left the place in a similar state many times when he was a kid.

Outside, the sea mist had thickened and the car park had faded into a milky dream. The night air was chilly and the whole place seemed suddenly gothic, threatening. A black and white film scene drifted across his consciousness, something from *Rebecca* or *The Night has Eyes*. Invisible waves dragged and bullied the shingle below them, accentuating the silence.

Framed in cameo against one of the car-park lights, the carpenter was pointing upwards, towards the gable. Lou's eyes took some time to adjust to the light, and he failed to identify the point of interest.

'What?' he said.

'Up there, the iron brackets,' said the carpenter.

Finally, Lou saw a couple of black metal arms

stretching out from the wall, with two rusty chains dangling from them.

Well?

'That was the sign,' said the carpenter, dropping his arm and turning to face him. 'A painting of Hotel Corvo with the rooks above it, real work of art. That's because I did it myself,' he grinned.

'So what happened to it?' Lou felt helpless now, aware that the story was being stretched to its limits for dramatic effect.

He got the full story inside, over a last foolish double – he knew that he'd suffer terribly in the morning.

When the men with the Irish accents had left Hotel Corvo it was dark, he was told. Everyone returned to their routines, the banter restarted and the place returned to normal, with Big M behind the bar, giving free drinks and fooling around. Pryderi had been leaning against the bar, said the carpenter, when there was an almighty bang and the whole place fell silent. Just the one explosion, but it shattered the peace at Hotel Corvo. Pryderi had swivelled round to look at the door and his face had gone all white. *Shotgun*, he said under his breath, and then louder, *that was a bloody shotgun*.

A barful of people froze, waiting for the next development. But silence returned to the clifftop and after a while Big M went outside to see what had happened. The first thing he saw was the hotel sign on the ground, peppered with shotgun pellets. After looking around to see if there was anyone there, he carried the sign inside and took it round the back, into their office. He and Pryderi made a joke of it, and the rest of the night passed uneventfully, but a big change arrived at Hotel Corvo when the next day dawned.

The mist had gone, but so had the customers. After that single gunshot the public had voted with their feet. Even the seven silhouettes had gone elsewhere, leaving Hotel Corvo alone, unloved, and completely empty. The place became a landlocked Marie Celeste, rusting away as the weeks became months.

Lou finished his drink and said goodnight to the

men. His bed was damp but he didn't care. He was asleep, slumped face down on the grubby sheets, before he could take his clothes off.

IV

Lou was back at his college desk, talking to his screen. He'd always hated Skyping people, it was so unreal and it made him feel odd. At the other end of the link was Colin Dorton, an English academic who'd helped him previously with the Big M story. But Dorton didn't want to play ball any more.

'For chrissakes get out of that Celtic scene, it's as dead as a doorknob,' Dorton was saying to him, a fraction of a second before his lips moved. He looked ghostly and blurred; someone from an old sci-fi series maybe. *Quatermass and the Pit*.

'Celtica's gone, it's dead and buried,' he was saying, as if to jangle Lou's nerves even further. 'Look to America, that's where it's at. You're nobody unless you've got an American angle. We're the fifty-first state, virtually. You've sidelined yourself, nobody'll take any notice of you, Lou.'

Later, after their chat, a gaping depression swallowed him. He hadn't felt like that for ages, not since the time he'd sat alone in his room for weeks during an awful episode when a student party had got out of hand; a girl had accused him of something, along the whisper lines, and he'd been ostracised. He'd felt very lonely, and he was feeling just as lonely today. Useless, too. He'd been beaten by the machine during seven consecutive games of Mahjong Titans and he'd become so frustrated he'd cheated with the H button to get his final clearance. Catrin seemed to have no problem with Mahjong Titans, she had a near hundred per cent record and all he could manage was a lousy twenty-two per cent win rate. If he was useless at Mahjong Titans, what else was he useless at without knowing it? How could he clear up the Big M thingy if he couldn't win a little computer game? He'd have to cheat all the way.

He was staring at his screen, and it had a new

picture on it, a view of Hotel Corvo which he'd taken with the light fading at dusk; this accentuated the dark green of the trees and the yellow lights in the hotel windows. His mouth suddenly tasted of whiskey, as if to remind him of his night there.

Dr Colin Dorton was right, probably. With the morning yawning before him, Lou felt isolated and lonely. He'd noticed already that without lectures to deliver and seminars to host he'd become detached from college life. History, language, literature – they were all to do with personal ambition and career paths, really. They seldom stayed pure. Academia had become a passive silence outside his door, tainted with the smell of irrelevant old books, and punctuated very rarely by the squeak of occasional shoes and distant banging doors. Life was passing him by. He'd made a mistake; revenge had led him up a blind alley. Lou was wasting away, emotionally and intellectually. His old colleagues still greeted him when they met, but since he was out of the loop now they left it at that. Dead in the water. He missed the gossip, arrivals and departures, the shagging news. A couple of new faces passed him with the vaguest of nods. Llwyd McNamara had messed up, career-wise. And his home life wasn't a barrel of laughs either; sidelined now by the later stages of pregnancy, he felt surplus to requirements there too.

Approaching the endgame, Catrin had gone off sex and spent most of the night reading Roth, Don DeLillo or Walter Abish by the light of her bedside lamp, as if to highlight her husband's error of judgement.

Black with self-loathing, Lou opened Feeney's second chapter. It resumed where the first had left off, with the gunshot at Hotel Corvo and its aftermath: all the clients had taken fright and disappeared into thin air. Pryderi had got involved with the IRA, or mobsters, or top-end loan sharks who'd felled the hotel sign with a single gunshot. The blast had echoed around the chough nests on the cliffs below, then a deep silence had arrived. Nary a soul had bothered them after that and the place had become a Welsh Jamaica Inn, habituated by four benighted humans and a barful of ghosts, all of them peering forlornly through grimy windows as thick sea mists obliterated the world outside. Salty little weeds struggled through widening cracks. Rust raced along the railings. Hotel Corvo, the most happening place in the county, had become the restaurant at the end of the universe. Dead, as dead as Lou's career. This was when all the staff had left; Lou had gone up to Oxford well before that and his ma had faded from his life.

The second chapter documented a bleak period in the history of Hotel Corvo. Dr Dermot Feeney had sailed across the Irish Sea to trace Big M's story during the great silence, and his morose tone matched perfectly the autumnal decline in the hotel's fortunes as the quartet waited for something to happen. But it never did.

Apparently Feeney's stay at a B&B near Hotel Corvo had been suitably mist-shrouded, as if the village had donned its own invisibility cloak and played dead among the damp, silvery spider webs which shone eerily in the encircling gorse. Feeney had been a big man with a bumpy face, corpulent and grumpy, looming along the coastal path in a huge gaberdine mac and a ridiculous leather bush hat. He grumbled in his notes that the food was poor and his bed damp. Service was virtually non-existent, glassware and cutlery dirty. But he'd managed to find one person who was prepared to talk to him. Lou knew that person – it was one of the seven Corvo regulars, the carpenter who'd taken him outside the hotel and showed him the shot-off sign. He'd been commissioned by Pryderi to paint a new sign for Hotel Corvo, and he'd visited the place to measure up and discuss the contract.

Without any customers, the four friends had locked up and closed all the shutters on the ground floor, which gave the place a wartime feel, bunker-ish and Frankensteinian. According to Feeney it had reminded Ziggy of a bad winter when she was a child, when snowdrifts had covered the ground floor windows of her home and partially blinded the place; downstairs at the hotel had been equally ghostly and other-worldly.

When spring came they'd started a vegetable

garden in the back and you could still see the potato ridges, but their hearts weren't in it and very little produce reached the kitchen. No, they'd lived with the gun and the rod, and of course the freezers were full of food which lasted for quite a while. They stayed there, in total seclusion, for a year, Pryderi ranging across the countryside with his shotgun, Big M looming out of a fog with an eight-pound bass dangling over his shoulder.

And so they lived on in that strange seething silence which envelops social pariahs. With the world erased, they'd sat outside daily at a table below a large green parasol with a white frill, drinking wine and picking at fish and rice dishes with the best silver service, discussing their slow activities outside Hotel Corvo: Pryderi stalking his prey and trying to come to terms with messing it all up; Big M, cool as ever, half-asleep on the rocks below as the shoals swarmed around him; Rhiannon on her horse, an occasional silhouette on the hill above them as she returned home; Ziggy stationed in a chintzy chair in a big bay window overlooking the sea, worried, drinking too much, overdressed and over-gilded, consumed by her husband's foolishness.

And when the sea mist thinned sometimes in the afternoon heat they'd find Big M sitting alone at the table outside, playing solo chess with his Lewis set, the board glistening with dampness and a hoar of tiny droplets covering him like icing sugar.

One year became two. They found honey from wild swarms and ate it with their hands, sweet golden liquid around their lips, in their hair, jewelling their worn shirts.

The carpenter disclosed in his statement to Feeney that one day, when he went to check up on them, he'd opened some of the freezers in the basement and they'd held some food still, though one of them revealed a sorrowful sight with a small pile of frozen prawn sachets stacked in one corner and a pile of frozen sprouts in another, indicating that no one much liked frozen prawns or sprouts. The bar was still relatively well stocked when they finally gave up and asked the carpenter to board up the windows. Pryderi, Big M, Rhiannon and Ziggy departed one lunchtime in Big M's vintage three-litre Bentley, with the top down. It was a fine, clear day: the first they'd experienced in ages.

But it wasn't a shortage of food which forced them to leave their island in the mist. It wasn't even a lack of booze. Maybe a shortage of human company played some part in it, but the main reason for their departure from Hotel Corvo was quite mundane. It was Big M's feet which propelled them onto the open road again.

One day, stooped over his chess set with one of the shrunken little figures in his hand, he'd looked up at Rhiannon and said: *We've got to go, girl. We've got to go.*

Dr Feeney had tried his hand at humour in describing this episode but he was a fish out of water when it came to levity. There was nothing particularly funny about it anyway. Rather sad, really. Big M had leant back in his chair and placed one of his famous feet on the table, displaying a battered leather shoe. Once it had been a bespoke, hand-stitched Saddle Oxford in light tan from John Lobb. Top of the range.

But Big M was down in the dumps, he'd had enough. His trademark shoes – his Ones and Twos, his Rhythm and Blues, his Scooby Doos were falling apart on his feet. Big M was down at heel, quite literally.

So what? said Pryderi, placing one of his own feet on the table and showing a cheap pair of black boots in equally poor condition. Inside one of his ribbed stockings they could see the familiar bulge of his compact Beretta 92. He was never without it these days.

Nah, said Big M. *We've got to go.*

After all he was a sex god, and sex gods didn't walk around in shit shoes.

Hotel Corvo was a big black hulk, a sunken liner sleeping with the fishes, when they drove away. Big M behind the wheel, Pryderi by his side, Ziggy and Rhiannon in the back. Old-fashioned style, women in bright summer dresses and chiffon scarves, a wicker hamper between them. Rhiannon leant forward, ran a hand through her lover's hair, and said *someone needs a haircut, loverboy.*

Some decent boots, that's all he hankered after. He longed for the creak and perfume of a new pair of leather shoes on his feet.

Pryderi was ready to go too. So tired now, he'd been continuously on edge since the gunshot. Bloodshot eyes, stubble. Nasty tremor when he held a young deer in his gunsights; he'd lost his nerve. Didn't want to shoot innocent animals any more either. He was superstitious: it could be him next in the firing line.

So where are you taking us, Twinkle Toes, he asked Big M.

But Big M didn't have a masterplan. Never had, really. Go with the flow, have a nice time, don't waste energy on trouble and strife. He didn't want any angst or head games. That's the way Big M lived his life. *Never collide with the modern world*, that's what he used to say. *Go round it, go under it, keep your head down till it's gone right past, but don't take it on head to head. It'll wear you down, sap your batteries, suck away your life juice.*

He just kept on driving along country roads,

keeping the afternoon sun behind him as it sank towards the western sea. Long ribbons of daisy-flecked grass flowed between the wheels. August was tired and sleepy, summer's sap-flow had slowed, and snails had already begun their long journey towards winter, climbing laboriously up the hogweed stalks; the season had come to a stop, a convoy waiting for its own spillage of pollen to be cleared off the road. Now it sat there in the spent grasses, its creaking bodywork already starting to rust.

They drove for hours, skirting deep woods squatting like huge green chiller cabinets, until the taller oaks and sycamores cast long shadows across the bleached wheatfields. They felt completely alone in this vast open terrain, and indeed they saw no one for a long time, not until late afternoon, when they met an England sign by the roadside. Shortly afterwards they entered a typical Hereford village, black and white cottages with sinister cats disappearing through rough holes under doors. Through the small-paned windows they could see warty hags with gnarled hands, up to no good behind broken cobwebs and piss-yellow net curtains.

For chrissakes carry on, said Ziggy, *or I'll start screaming.*

So on they went, following the signs for Hereford. They got there late at night when the light was failing, so hardly anyone saw them putting in at one of the better hotels, a place with a garage to hide away the car. Like so many bankrupts, Pryderi had a surprising ability to find tons of money when he needed to. He showed off, hinted at a secret stash, got them an expensive suite. Swiss bank account, or maybe not, wink wink. Rhiannon was taken aback and stayed close to Big M; she liked it all above board.

They stayed in this place for a month, keeping a low profile, making sure they spoke good English always. Posh place with plenty of toffs floating around. In the meantime, Pryderi used his hunter's instincts to comb the town for a bargain, and soon he'd spotted one – a boarded-up pub by the river called The Saddle Inn, going for a song. The previous landlord had been a dipso who'd played the optics all day, pissed as a rat by noon, people helping themselves while he picked fights with strangers. Nightmare, the place had been closed down by the constabulary.

So Pryderi bought it with his back pocket dosh and the four of them threw themselves into the business. Nice coat of blue paint, clean windows, yellow chintz curtains, classy prints on the walls, tables and chairs outside and a nice bistro feel to the place; shiny beer taps, good coffee, relaxing view of the old Wye Bridge. Felt almost French. Big M used to go down to the river each morning for a dip.

I just love that river, he'd say. *Rises in Wales, ends in Wales, takes a stroll through England along the way. The water sounds Welsh, it so reminds me of home.*

You'd know where he was by his dragon-red towelling robe on the bank, weighed down by the finest blue suede shoes ever seen in the city. Elvis would have been proud of them; a pair of catalogue Ben Shermans with a price tag to match their mod origins in the sixties: a mere sixty-five quid. He'd thrown them in as extras during a big splurge, but once on his feet they'd stayed there. Those shoes became his trademark.

Big M, with his usual aplomb, opened a nice little restaurant at the back.

The customers poked fun at him, they said *shuffle them shoes Big M*, but he liked that sort of thing.

The Ben Shermans looked a little out of place beneath his checkerboard trousers, but his chef's toque seemed to balance things out once he'd added a blue flash to the headband. Nice touch, a hint of cavalier humour. They liked him, they liked his little eatery hidden away at the end of a flowerpot alley, with its little courtyard, fountain, and abundant greenery. He grew a splendid moustache and twiddled it as he engaged in badinage, teasing the men, making ridiculous passes at the women – all of them, indiscriminately, even the grandmothers: he was a natural magical realist. He went to their tables at dusk with rosebuds in slender vases, he lit their cigarettes, he indulged in crazy episodes of tap dancing as he carried the plates, he sang Tyrolean love songs from the windows above, he even brought out his fiddle on special occasions, swept around the place playing gypsy music and ogling the ladies close up with incredibly mournful eyes.

And the food, ah, the food was out of this world. Seafood a house speciality, but the *à la carte* menu was huge and catholic, a high church liturgy for a swelling congregation. It was just a hobby to Big M; just another string to his bow. But he was booked up every night, and soon enough he'd garnered a Michelin star and a great review in the *Sunday Times*. The chief ape himself, A.A. Gill, had declared that the food was much too good to be served so proximate to the dark ugly trolls who lurked just over the border.

And so it went on, a new paradise on earth was created by the four of them, but it didn't go on for long enough. That old human worm, envy, crawled around the gutters of Hereford and spoke in many ears, whispering, *who is this man who wears his blue suede shoes in bed, seduces your wives and daughters, wriggles his hips and says he's a love god? Why do our burghers crowd his tables, laugh in his sunny courtyard, go home with their wives to love again after years of cold indifference?*

Soon, a brick sailed through one of the front windows. A few scenes occurred in the courtyard, staged by paid thugs. It was happening all over again, but no threatening gunshot was needed this time round. Customers were melting away and worse was to come, said the rumours. Bad stuff: a knife in the dark, or fire through the letterbox. Pryderi stowed his Beretta in his sock again. Ziggy started to chain smoke. Rhiannon doodled pictures of horses on napkins and dropped plates in the kitchen. It couldn't go on.

Pryderi was mad with rage. He wanted to fight fire with fire; he wanted to take them on at their own game. He prodded Big M, urged him on with fighting talk. But to no avail. Big M wasn't having any of it, his fighting days were over. *Last thing I need is a spell in the cooler.* Maybe he was ready for a change anyway. Cooking all day could get boring, and there wasn't much time to chill. Big M spread his hands wide, shrugged his shoulders, and said: 'Let's move on. What's the point? Trouble breeds trouble, anyway I've had enough of small-town people with small-town minds. The river's getting colder, autumn's on the way. Let's crack on, let's have a nice easy time for a while, let's see some places and watch the leaves fall.'

Infuriated, Pryderi gave in, sold the place for a song, and had the Bentley serviced.

Soon they were gone.

Lou read the story till his eyes ached, then went for lunch in the students' caff downstairs. Tray in hand, he looked around for someone to sit with, but all eyes seemed to be elsewhere, anywhere except where he was standing. Again he felt isolated, and soon he was morose too. His sandwich tasted artificial and his too-hot coffee came in a styro-mug. Nothing felt real any more. Even the students around him had an ersatz quality about them, a submissive *Stepford Wives* blandness. Perhaps they were the Stepford children. Modern education had reduced the world to twelve incontrovertible bullet points, and the rest of the universe fitted neatly onto a Facebook page. Any restlessness was quickly numbed by a limitless flow of celebrity trivia. Christ, it was depressing. But he himself was a product of the same system. How much more exacting were *his* methods? Not nearly as good as Dr Dermot Feeney's, who'd actually gone out and found some of Big M's relatives. Yes, he'd got the story straight from the horse's mouth. Or maybe the cat's. Feeney had traced one of Big M's cousins, through a nostalgia forum called Manx for the Memories, to an old people's home in Douglas, Isle of Man. A geriatric who wore spanking new tartan slippers with gold bobbles, and who still had an interest in *lurve.*

Lou left half a sandwich and took his coffee to his room, then read on.

After Hereford, anonymity. Four chameleons in search of a shadow. Even Feeney wasn't allowed to know where they'd landed. **A city in England, never revealed*, said his notes. This time they rented a closed-down pub called The Shield and Dagger. Its cider specialties – Three Hammers, Green Goblin, Frosty Jack, Total Wipeout – hinted at a West

Country location. Glastonbury Tor in the distance, maybe. A house for hard-drinking men with silvery eyes, blinded young by the apple maggot.

Who knows where they went, because they kept themselves to themselves. No food this time. No showmanship from Big M, not for a while anyway. But eventually the Big M within got the better of him. What started as bar-room banter became a regular routine, which became a comedy slot every Friday night – Big M with a black hat and a mic, a spotlight, and a flow of rough cider. He'd developed a bit of a drink problem during that period, according to Feeney. Big M seemed to get better with every pint. Like the brew, he became even more potent and deadly as the night wore on. Friday night got to be very popular at the Mutton, as it was called, mutton dagger being a well-known synonym in those parts for a man's best friend...

The Shield and Dagger became a magnet as the Friday night comedy store spilled over into Saturday, then Sunday; taxis arrived suddenly from far and wide as Big M and his guests turned every weekend into a mini fringe event fuelled by gallons of scrumpy. His favourite routine, *Fill yer Boots*, based on his own penchance for snazzy footwear, was legendary. *Hell for Leather* also did very well. He was ideally suited to stand-up; cool and laconic, sad and ironic. But his popularity had the usual downside, and soon enough his success was pissing off all the local publicans. Their empty bars gave them plenty of time to work up a fury, and to plan revenge. One night the fab four at the Shield and Dagger were woken by a tremendous wall-rattling bang, and when the men opened the front door, Pryderi with his Beretta at the ready, they found a stinky old boot nailed to the wood, its tongue lolling out at them; inside it they found a message with an unlit match sellotaped to it. Not very polite. Pryderi put his Beretta back in his sock and read it.

The shits, he said to Big M without looking up. *They want us out of town by noon on Sunday. Or the place'll go up in smoke, us lot with it.*

He put the note back inside the boot and returned upstairs slowly, mumbling savagely to himself. Again he wanted to take them on, fight them, use the gun if necessary.

But Big M packed away his clothes and his fancy boots, cancelled all deliveries, and invited everyone in the town to a drink-till-we're-dry comedy session at the Mutton.

When they drove away at noon on Sunday – the timing was meant to be ironic – they left a pile of sleeping bodies and a hundred hangovers lying around in the Shield and Dagger. They left a message on the bar: *Lock up when you go and throw away the key.* The fun times were over. Yet again they said farewell to their temporary beds and hit the road.

Never mind, said Big M, *it was fun while it lasted.*

But Pryderi was getting pissed off with Big M's attitude, fed up with their gypsy lifestyle and fed up with being constantly hassled. Just because they were good at what they did. Or was it something else? Their accents? Maybe Big M's bed-seeking missiles, his wandering shoes?

Forget it, said Big M nonchalantly, driving the Bentley with his fingertips. He'd kept the comedy hat; it went well with his black Torino boots from Samuel Windsor, both soles studded with a single drawing pin to give a satisfying clink whenever Big M strode forwards. Vain, yes of course he was vain. But aren't we all, in different ways?

Jesus Christ, we can't go on like this, Pryderi had said in a roadside diner somewhere between the nowhere of their past and the nowhere of their future. *We can't go on like this.* He was looking at the clouds far off on the eastern horizon, and trying to eat a leathery breakfast which was vile enough to kill a dog. Those clouds – perhaps they should head towards them like storm hunters: perhaps they should ride into a tornado and end it all. Pryderi was feeling lower than he'd ever felt before, and the sky seemed higher. The world outside seemed vast and dark and threatening. Where next?

Lou stopped reading, went over to his window, and looked out onto the world again. The clouds were still there, a long line of them, but they were losing their shape and morphing into pale discolourations.

He thought of the computer clouds, viewed by four wandering friends sitting inside a grubby roadside diner. It was amazing how his mind could flick between the real world in front of him and the tiny world inside his computer. And there was yet another bank of clouds: those inside his head, on which rested the gods of the ancient world. Apollo, Lord of Mice, still alive in the small soft memories of mankind. God of the sun, truth and prophecy. A contradictory god, created in man's image; a beautiful smooth-skinned god, androgynous and bisexual, who could bring plague and then its antidote, healing. Lou tried to compare the four travellers in the roadside diner to the mythical mice which lived below Apollo's altar. He saw Pryderi as a mouse whose fate awaited him like a sprung trap; Big M was a small sleek mouse with a nose for cats. Yes, Big M was the master-mouse who found the next big grain store, then led his tribe to safety when the pied piper arrived.

His mind drifted to some of the mice events in his life; camping in the Lake District with his brother one Easter, with frost on the ground and a posse of Hell's Angels in the field below them, Lou had leant a bottle of milk against a fencing post before turning in, and when he tried to pour some milk into their tea mugs in the morning he'd wondered why the flow was so sluggish, until he saw a small mousy face, eyes closed for evermore, floating to the top of the cream: it had climbed in and drowned in the night. The mouse had looked like a tiny hairy child coming to the surface after a dive.

Lou turned back to his desk and read the last part of the chapter hurriedly, so that he could go home to Catrin. She wanted the nursery finished, ready for their baby.

Chapter M2 had been finished while Dr Feeney recovered at a Sligo clinic, his illness unspecified. Perhaps other things had started to go wrong in advance of his heart attack. Lou sympathised with him briefly, a big sick man alone in a strange bed, his heavy bushtracker's hat in his locker, sweat-stained and smelling like a newly flensed animal hide. One of

Lou's colleagues, who'd met Feeney at a convention, had described him as a quiet, brooding, sit-at-the-back man with acne scars and permanently mis-shaven features. But Feeney was cunning; he'd been able to follow the fab four on their fugitive journey thanks to a letter sent by Rhiannon to Pryderi a few years later when she was in a psychiatric unit. Her letter had been an attempt at catharsis – apparently her son had been taken into care for a while when he was a small child. But though never really meant to be seen by Pryderi, or by anyone else for that matter, the letter had been kept in the family archive.

Following their mournful meal at the roadside diner they'd headed off at a tangent, deep into Middle England, and when the people and houses passing by had changed almost beyond recognition they stopped the car at a country town and sat in it for a while, windows open, listening. By now they were far away from the sea, and far away too from the chiff-chaff cadence of their native country. The voices around them had slowed and stiffened, more clay now than sand. They could go no further; they had reached the end of the road.

This time it was Ziggy who took control.

No more bloody pubs, she said with feeling. The boys had messed up every time so far, so the girls would have a go. Something different. She left them sitting in the car and took a shufty down the high street. When she returned she had two bags of condensed cholesterol from the pie & cake shop, delicious sausage rolls still warm from the oven and fresh cream cakes. Mmm. Crumbs everywhere. Worth travelling for. So a pie & cake shop was out of the question, she said wryly. How about a shoe shop? She hadn't spotted one, they could sell some leather goods like bags and belts as well as footwear. Anything except cider. The smell of it made her sick now. And she'd heard stories of dead rats and all sorts of shit floating in the vats. Ziggy was all woman. She wanted a shoe shop.

You making fun of me? asked Big M, looking down at a pair of brand new boots on his size twelves.

No, said Ziggy, *I've just seen some of the most*

down-at-heel plebs in the whole wide world. Bloody peasants. We'll educate them, give them a better class of footwear.

Quite a snob, Ziggy. Who was *she* to look down on people? said Big M. After all, she was an itinerant without a home or a job. That shut her up. But shoe shop it was.

As the other patients recovered and went home, Dermot Feeney had documented it all from his clinic. Superstitious, he'd started to fear the three empty beds swimming in shark circles around him, their cold white sheets hunting for fresh meat.

Ziggy rented a shop in the high street and dipped into Pryderi's back pocket to fund her new venture. Cider and comedy had served them well, he had wads of cash again. While the shop was being fitted out they sent Big M on a mission to buy the classiest boots in Britain. Brown, black, red, blue or gold, they would have to be the best available. Big M relished his task and set off in the Bentley, happy to be alone again. When he returned, a fortnight later, he was sporting an amazing pair of Lazarus Python winklepickers from Paolo Vandini, which Rhiannon ordered him to remove at once. Unusually for her she was short of patience with his sang froid, his come-day go-day attitude. Big M was always sunny side up, forever paddling in the warm river of his own life. A shrug of the shoulders and then the boyish smile, disarming everyone. But it was time to be a bit more serious; they were attracting the wrong sort of attention again.

So Big M went into a bit of a sulk and spent his days hanging around bars, while Pryderi went all macho on them and refused to *mince around in a poofter parlour* as he put it. Still, the shop was a big success and Big M was kept busy supplying it with top-class footwear. Ziggy insisted on calling it *Gracious in Defeat.*

The shop sign, white lettering on purple, was revolting but the plebs loved it. As autumn blew its first crinkle-cut leaves down the high street the populace lined up to part with their Jobseeker's Allowance. Big M spent many days and nights away buying eye-boggling boots and staying at expensive hotels. He'd hand his card to the bar girls and introduce himself humorously as *chief buyer* to a shoe empire called *Gracious in Defeat.* Wit and shoes: with just one more ingredient, chocolate, he introduced a whole new meaning to infidelity.

But success came at a price, as per usual. In the same way as Hay-on-Wye became a book town, Ziggy's success turned the town around *Gracious in Defeat* into a shoe-shop sensation. The new shops arrived overnight, menacing the walkways with rack after rack of cut price footwear. *Moccasin Mecca.* Then came *Cobblers!* Afterward they arrived in droves: *The Athlete's Foot, Shutopia, R. Soles, Sock 'n Sole, Footloose and Fancyfree, The Shoe Must Go On, Sole Proprietor, Walk on the Wild Side...*

Soon the town seemed to offer nothing except shoe shops and charity shops selling second-hand shoes to a shoe-obsessed population.

Just wait, said Big M, *we'll be getting a brick through the window any day now.*

He acquired a couple of low-maintenance dogs to warn of intruders in the night, two jet-black terriers which he named Left and Right in a sardonic reference to the little bootees they sold to teach tots their left from their right. And when he returned from one of his buying missions, sure enough he was met by a boarded-up window, splinters of glass on the pavement and three very glum faces sitting upstairs in the living quarters. The rest is history, as they say. After the inevitable sale came the inevitable escape. Once again Pryderi wanted to put up a fight. But once again Big M said nothing, packed his stuff and slept in the Bentley until they were all ready to join him. A week later they were on the road again, this time heading back towards Wales. They'd had enough of the English blowing hot and cold on their ventures. God knows how long it took them to sight Hotel Corvo and the cliffs of West Wales again, but when they did it was a blessed relief, however derelict the hotel looked.

Lou closed the chapter and moved it to the recycle bin, ready for deletion. After a short examination of his desktop picture he decided it was time for a change, the photo of Hotel Corvo was beginning to depress him. He'd have to take another pic. In the meantime he flicked through the folder of alternative screensavers which came with the computer. One of them showed an autumnal scene by a lake. It looked like somewhere in Canada, though he'd never been to North America: he was merely responding to previous pictures he'd seen of lakes in Canada. That was globalisation for you. Instead he selected a photo of a field: a generic, undulating tract of greenness with a blue sky above it. A bit bland, really, good on the eye but meaningless. That was the way of the world.

Lou closed down his computer and went to stand by the window, in what had become a nightly adieu to the scene outside, a vista which he increasingly liked and admired. Roof ridges reddened below him when the sun set, purple and mauve slates glinted whenever it rained; he loved the narrow estuary with its flotilla of colourful fishing boats, the broad sea beyond, the distant islands and headlands, and towering above it all, the mountains. Perhaps he would take a picture of the scene tomorrow, or on the first fine day, and put it on his desktop. But wouldn't that be odd, since the view was always there for him? How could he capture the essence of the place, its numen – the picture behind the mirror? He imagined a ghostly assembly of matter constantly forming and reforming behind the glass facades of mirrors everywhere around the world; a secret alternative world of almost-images. Did some people leave more of themselves behind mirrors than others? Surely Big M did. If Lou was supposed to breathe in molecules from Julius Caesar or whoever on a daily basis, how many molecules from Big M were there floating around in the world? A lot, thought Lou. He was beginning to like the bloke. Why was he trying to obliterate him, anyway? What was the issue?

Lou examined the horizon, now without a vestige of clouds, and went back to his desk. After restarting his computer he put all three chapters in the recycle bin and pulled the plug on them. *Was he sure?* asked the machine. *Yes he bloody well was*, answered Lou with his mouse. Finito. His revenge motive had lost its attraction so he would cut and run before it was too late, before he'd spent too much time on the project. And by killing off Dermot Feeney's magnum opus he'd queer the pitch for anyone else.

Lou checked the green memory stick and it was empty. Micro-dust would be gathering on the empty desks and chairs inside its miniature world; someone's lunchbox would be lying there with a titchy banana beginning to mould over (at this point his eyes flitted to his own fruit bowl); maybe there would be a pile of virtual junk mail clogging up the main vestibule. In the corner by the reception desk he imagined a family of microscopic woodlice in a huddle, becalmed, their robotic segments glinting dully in the pale afterlight of a nuclear winter.

Lou closed his computer again and prepared to leave for home. He'd pop over to the professor's room in the morning and realign his project; he'd say that Dermot Feeney's work was useless, the product of a diseased mind etc. His Skype conversation with Colin Dorton had given him a new direction. Perhaps he could compare Welsh literature in the end days of the Roman Empire to Welsh literature in the end days of the American empire; there were distinct similarities. As he prepared to go home he realised that he'd lost his car keys, and it was raining. He stood in the main vestibule for a while, wondering what to do. Then he walked quickly downwards through the darkening town, towards the taxi rank.

Travelling home, he watched the raindrops as they followed their strange cometic paths along the glass, and he thought of Dermot Feeney's words slipping one by one into the void.

V

Lou knocked on the door and heard a faraway voice. When he entered, the professor was standing at the only window, facing the outside world and looking out over the sea.

'Seems to be an important part of academic life,' said Lou to the professor's back.

'What's that?'

'Looking out through windows,' said Lou. 'I seem to do quite a lot of it myself.'

The prof turned towards him and released his hands from behind his back, then waved Lou towards a seat. Professor Williams had an aesthetic goatee, neatly trimmed, and a fine fall of perfectly white hair cascading backwards onto his shoulders. He looked every inch the part. Lou had long since wondered if the Professor Williamses of this world became academics because they looked like academics, or whether they became academics because they wanted all the visual trappings which went with the job. Lou was reminded of the Jehovah's Witness who called on him every month; he was convinced she'd become a Witness because her headscarf, her serf's appleskin face, her belted brown gaberdine, dense nylon stockings, oedema-bloated legs and open-toed white sandals were so archetypically suited to her role.

Lou started his preamble but got no further than the opening line before the prof interrupted. Lou winced because he'd sounded like a Witness himself, standing on someone's doorstep, getting ready to make a pitch.

'Ah, the Big M project,' said Professor Williams, professorially. 'Great timing, I've got something for you. Nearly forgot about it.'

He swivelled, opened a drawer, scrabbled around in it, closed it, then went through every drawer in the desk before exclaiming theatrically; Lou watched him prance towards a brown enamel jug with a lustrous blue band, sitting on an upper bookshelf.

'Should've remembered, I always put them in here,' he said, before sitting down again and plonking something on the desk between them. He kept his hand over it, protectively, while he explained its history.

'Sent to me anonymously through the post, not even a note,' said the prof, but his cunning blue eyes said otherwise. Lou felt a chill wind blowing through him. Something odd was happening. He was being set up; he felt it in his bones. Forces far beyond his control were moving outside the windows of the college. He was just a pawn in the game, he could sense it now. Suddenly he felt very small. Alone in one of those tiny deserted rooms in the green memory stick, waiting for the tannoy voice.

Professor Williams moved his hand and revealed a memory stick, identical to the one in Lou's fruit bowl, but this one was red instead of green. Uncanny. Lou had anticipated what was coming, except for the colour difference.

'Medical records,' said the prof. 'Illuminating. Very little mention of Big M as far as I could see, though I didn't look right through it. But Pryderi's all over the place. Didn't know he'd been inside a loony bin, that's a new one on me.'

Lou studied the memory stick, then picked it up off the desk. It seemed heavier than the green one. He enjoyed its smoothness in the dry dock of his hand, a tiny caravel, freshly come into harbour from a voyage of discovery. Perhaps he should give them names like Nina and Pinta – but that would imply a third, the Santa Maria: battered little ships with cargoes of knowledge (or misinformation) in their holds instead of yams and coconuts and gold. He examined the vessel's interior and imagined the invisible chambers of his newly acquired microworld.

Professor Williams anticipated his next question.

'Why us? No idea Llwyd, no idea at all. Someone must have heard about your research, someone who wanted the true story told perhaps. Or someone with a grudge? Agenda? Your guess is as good as mine, Llwyd. Make what you will of it.'

And with that it became clear that Professor Williams wanted him gone.

'By the way,' he added as Lou made his way towards the door. 'You've disappeared off the radar. Someone asked me who you were the other day, seems you're invisible. Perhaps you need to get out more.'

Lou nodded sharply and closed the door a little too firmly.

His room seemed smaller when he returned to it. But he felt glad that the view from his window was grander, more sublime than the view from Professor Williams' room. His own view took in the estuary, the coastal strip and the mountains as well as distant headlands and an offshore island. The prof's view was less interesting: a panorama of the sea and little else. The prof's view was a captain's view as he steered his ship towards new lands, whereas Lou's view was a pioneer's view, the vista from a newly erected log cabin on an alien shore.

Now, back inside his cabin, he contemplated his

fate, for he felt absolutely sure that he was being observed and manipulated – yes, cued up like a ball on a snooker table. And he felt utterly helpless, because he was effectively bound and gagged by the constraints of his project. Was he part of a social experiment? Or was academia exerting its customary vice-like grip on history?

The prof's steely blue eyes had betrayed him, but Lou suspected that the strings were being pulled by someone else. By the politicans maybe, who might be looking – as per usual – for a precedence to justify a pogrom or a power grab. Modern history wasn't a beautiful construct made of stainless steel and glass; it was a tatty boxful of cold plasticine rolled into childish shapes by a classroom of idiot children who had long ago merged all the different political colours into one grey mass. Lou would have to be careful now. His every move was being watched. He felt like a sheep being chanelled through different pens towards the final abattoir chamber.

After a few minutes of thought by his window he stabbed the new memory stick into his computer and moused its contents onto the desktop. Just the one document this time, an official-looking report with the name of a West Wales hospital underscored with warnings about privacy and access. It was a mental assessment, and the client was one Pryderi Jones. There was something pornographic about ogling a man's state of mind many years after the event; a man in a state of absolute vulnerability, sitting in a closed room with strangers. It was easy for Lou to enter the memory stick and pass through its wormholes. He'd been inside a psychiatric unit himself, many times. As a visitor of course, wandering through corridors where time had congealed into a thick albumen inside the nestbound eggs of mental illness.

Nowadays most modern psychiatric units nestled close to the main regional hospital, and Lou thought of them as latter-day leper huts, huddled by a wayside church. The inmates he saw as pilgrims shuffling towards the holy grail of sanity, fooled by yet another chimera. If religion had been a serum self-administered by the poor and sick to bring on numbing bouts of fatalism, then modern psychiatry was no more than a rodeo with fancy-dressed cowboys trying to herd and brand a few enraged steers let loose below the blinding high-noon sun of madness. You could smell the fear of those poor creatures, penned in their pastel-painted corrals, jabbed at by overpaid psychiatrists as they entered the arena.

Lou padded down a silent corridor inside the memory stick. Piss and Fear and Factor X. The same smells pervaded psychiatric units all over the land. Almost every inmate left his sense of humour at the door, as shoes might be left outside a mosque. The rituals were high church – pills as communion wafers, TV cables removed and taken to the sacred office like vestments at the end of each neverending day. Papal visits by consultants; ex cathedra pronouncements on psychiatric mantras. Food trays with indents to match each course, every hymn having its allotted place in the service.

Lou searched inside the memory stick, read its testimony, and encountered various scenes within. A young man talked animatedly to the hot water geyser in a kitchen, his half-made mug of tea filming over on the sink before him. A dark, beautiful young woman journeyed between the tables, perfecting one of her wonderful fables of paranoia. A small sallow woman, pickled in alcohol and little more than a shrunken ju-ju head, sat in a chair by the television, smelling of vodoo rites and chicken feathers.

Lou turned a corner in the rose-coloured gloom of the memory stick and started travelling away from the centre. A short, stout man with a florid face and a mournful moustache thudded past him without looking up. The bland carpetscape became so boring that Lou started to notice dead spiders curled up in corners, and a cobweb of hairline cracks in the paintwork.

He reacted badly to the kitsch on the walls – paintings donated by village art clubs and landscapes churned out by amateur photographers, scenes from a forever beautiful, idealised country on the other side of the compound wall, as if to stress the inmates' isolation. Then he arrived at a small, oddly shaped room where three corridors collided; there was a table and some chairs, a dishevelled magazine rack, and some half-hearted foliage which was probably repro. A set of French windows, slightly ajar, led to a garden set inside the belly of the unit, surrounded on all sides by a high Legoland of bricks and wall-eyed windows.

It was a strange little garden, concentric with benches around its outer rim, interspersed with bay trees and flower tubs; then there was an inner courtyard protected by a high raised bed of flowers, mostly nasturtiums, whose riotously happy orange looked rather manic. Inside all this, like a bosse on a shield, lay a miniature gold-coloured fountain with a faux marble lip on which two people were seated, facing each other. Lou was reminded of a Victorian painting, Alma-Tadema's *Ask Me No More* perhaps. A trickle of unenthusiastic water ululated softly as it throbbed in the pipehead. Lou studied the scene. A man with a certain brooding presence was slouched with one haunch on the marble, his other leg jutting out for balance. A woman was stooped over him and they seemed to be conversing, but then Lou realised that the woman was the only one talking. The man, who was large and powerful with a mess of hair, sat there listening, with his head bowed. He looked like an exhausted rugby player sitting in the changing room after an unexpected drubbing – and that's what he was, in a way, because Pryderi had once been the pride of Welsh rugby. The woman had a mop in her hand, and she appeared to be a cleaner. Her free hand rested for a while against his unshaven cheek, before moving up to play with his hair. They seemed to be on the verge of intimacy, had Pryderi not been so distracted. She moved off, leaving him alone. Occasionally he raised a mug to his mouth, but then he seemed to fall into a reverie and the mug became glued to his lips.

Lou entered this garden secreted inside the memory stick and sat down on one of the outer benches, well away from the fountain, though he could see by now that it was a cheap garden-centre version. Doubtless it was lit up at night in a selection of lurid colours. The French windows opened and a young man walked up to Pryderi, spoke to him soothingly and prised the mug from his hand. After a little coaxing he guided Pryderi down the path, towards the corridors. Lou sat still and let them brush past him; he got an inquiring look from the nursing attendant, but Pryderi's eyes seemed dead to the world, fixed on a trouble spot a few inches in front of him. The poor bloke had evidently suffered a breakdown; the skin on his face was flaking badly and his mouth had lost its shape. Lou noticed another disturbing sight: Pryderi's pants were damp around the crotch and seat, though this may have been caused by the fountain. Still inside the memory stick, Lou followed them through the intestines of the unit, until they reached a side room where a small assembly of people sat waiting. An invisible, indiscernible badge or colouring marked them out as staff members, as a hawkmoth's markings might distinguish it from a lacewing. Then someone saw the state of Pryderi's pants and he was whisked away to be changed. It was clear that a meeting was about to take place, so Lou left the scene and returned to his room at the college. On his screen he could see a mental health assessment form filled in by Pryderi's case worker, probably one of the moth people in the side room.

It started with a synopsis of Pryderi's general appearance on the day of admission. The person who'd compiled the report had a young, naive style which noted that Pryderi had been in a right old state, dirty and smelly, when he arrived at the unit. No shoes on his feet, in need of a haircut. He was physically unresponsive, withdrawn, and unwilling or unable to speak. He'd sat in his chair, head down, mute.

The assessment in the memory stick tried to describe his condition by using a number of different criteria under sub headings.

General appearance
Looks like he's been in a rugby match, earth and mud stains all over his clothes, moss and leaves and bits of briar sticking to him. Face very sad. Movements slow and directionless. Social interaction nil.

Speech
Mr Jones hasn't spoken since arrival.

Mood
Distressed while in the company of people, insists on being alone. Self-absorbed and inactive when on his own in the garden or in the quiet room, hasn't been in the dayroom and will only eat alone. Avoids all social interaction.

Thinking
Unknown, but he seems very depressed.

Perception
Unknown, since he won't communicate.

Cognition
Ditto.

Insight
Ditto.

Judgement
Ditto.

General remarks
Very little can be ascertained about Mr Jones, since he won't communicate. He seems to be in a state of shock, and insists on being completely alone wherever he is in the building. He likes quiet places. When he first arrived he was accompanied by a man who refused to give his name. They had two small dogs with them. According to a doctor in casualty, both men had been walking in the countryside when their dogs became involved in a fight with a badger. When the dogs became trapped in the sett, Mr Jones started to dig down with his hands in an attempt to rescue them but he was bitten by the badger, so his friend flagged down a passing ambulance so that he could come in for a tetanus jab. This friend brought Mr Jones to the psychiatric unit because he went into a rigid state and appeared to be suffering a breakdown.

This other man mentioned something about a gunshot, though there were no injuries. The porter on main entrance said the dogs were a bit manic and actually entered the unit for a while. Both men appeared to be distressed and wild in appearance – the porter thought they were gypsies or homeless people. But according to the ambulance driver the men flagged him down near a cliff-top hotel and asked to be brought to the hospital. The picture is unclear, but hopefully we'll get to the bottom of it when someone visits Mr Jones, though it's been over a week since he arrived and no one has come yet.

Health

Blood tests show no physical problems except mild anaemia (iron tablets prescribed, dietary advice has been sent to the caterers). Bruising and contusions have healed. Please note – he has a rare blood group, RH negative.

> *Possessions*
> Huge roll of money (which he won't part with!)
> Memory stick (green, transparent, which he also insists on keeping)
>
> *Clothing etc*
> He has been issued with an emergency outfit and a pair of trainers, plus toothbrush and plastic razors, soap etc. He has refused to wear the trainers and remains unshaven, though he has been cleaned up.

Lou sat back in his seat and put his head in his hands. A green memory stick! Could it be the same one? Had Dr Dermot Feeney somehow got his hands on it and claimed its valuable cargo as his own? Had Dr Feeney been a latter-day wrecker who'd lanterned Pryderi's ship of memories onto the rocks and then claimed it as salvage? Or had he merely stolen it from an academic vault? This possibility gave a strange, surreal twist to the plot, since it was becoming almost impossible for Lou to source the material arriving at his door. Some of the info was probably true, but some of it might have been introduced as a series of palimpsests by someone with an agenda. But who, and why? Was the story important enough to be used by someone as a propaganda tool? There was a possibilty, of course, that Pryderi and Big M had been part of something much bigger, and their rugby fame had been used as a cover. Yes, that was a distinct possibility, thought Lou. If the state or the church were involved, as per usual, then Pryderi and Big M – who had been heroes of their time – could have been very useful. But who had swiped the memory stick from Pryderi – had it been the very person who'd written the hospital report all those years ago, a person who was just another pawn in the game, someone who was little more than an office clerk? Lou cursed himself for wiping the green memory stick; he fetched it from the fruit bowl and wiped a smudge of dead banana off it, then pushed it into its docking bay and moused it open. Nothing. Sweet FA, as he'd feared. He checked his recycling bin and that too was empty. Idiot. He'd destroyed everything, but why? He saw a picture of himself on the deck of the Irish ferry, tossing sheaves of paper into the sea and chuckling drunkenly. Evil little goblin. What had driven him to do that? Some senseless wish to get his own back, but on whom? He could dredge up a shoal of excuses. Was it Pryderi's swaggering manliness, which contrasted so strongly with his own nerdy insustantiability? Or was it the possibility that Big M was his father and had abandoned him – after all, there was a definite likeness around the eyes, he'd seen it in the photos on the walls of the Hotel Corvo. Yes, there was a big vengeful worm eating Lou's insides, as big as one of those hideous Indian tapeworms.

Had he really come from the tall, handsome, easy-going man who had stared back at him from the uniform wooden frames? A man with a passion for classy women and fancy shoes? Those pictures, like the landscapes on the walls of the psychiatric unit, were snapshots from the country's fabled past. They were instant forms of propaganda, perpetuating ancient myths and portraying a green country, beautiful and honourable, filled to bursting with heroes and lovely women living according to ancient codes of honour, courteous and moral and honest. Civilised people, with fine sensibilities and unusual abilities, aesthetic and brilliant. Propaganda, all of it. And look at Wales now. An old country overwhelmed by a digital tide of cultural effluence, living in a virtual world imported and manipulated by rich and powerful men. A nation numbed by capitalism, trussed up and ready to be eaten at leisure by the all-consuming mega-corps which had spun their huge nets between the hedge funds of the world. Lou felt sick with hatred, hatred for everything that man had done to the world. He closed down his computer and prepared to go home, then went over to his window and stood there in his coat, still seething, looking at the lights coming on in the streets below him. Above him, the stars were coming out; he could see Deneb emerging as the Summer Triangle slid towards deep autumn. The world outside felt huge and dark and damply wonderful, an enormous copse with a bristling, aggressive super-badger passing through its undergrowth, snuffling and tearing at the ground; it was during brief moments such as this that the human animal saw how small and transient he was. Perhaps such moments were becoming rarer; blanked out by white light, the universe was gradually fading from sight. Man's urban chaos was a huge props department which had become hopelessly cluttered, reducing the human drama to a wait in the wings for seven billion extras as a group of political fools worked on their broken *deus ex machina*.

Standing there, Lou's idling mind came up with something. Hadn't he noticed that the red stick had forty kilobytes of memory stored on it, whilst the Pryderi document couldn't possibly account for all of that? There had to be something else on it. He decided to look at it in the morning, then changed his mind and sat down at his desk again, still in his coat. Whilst he fired up his computer he phoned home to tell Catrin he'd be late, but there was no response, which was strange because there was no reason on earth why she shouldn't be there. Unless, of course, she'd gone into labour. As he sat there watching his screensaver appear he realised that he should be doing more, so he tried her mobile, again without result. That was really strange.

He knew he should be going out in search of her, but he continued with the operation. He was thinking now about the baby inside her, a tiny charioteer about to enter a mad coliseum. Lou had been excited about the birth, but as it came nearer he'd detected an ambivalence within himself: a classical Freudian complex perhaps, a realisation that a usurper was about to claim his kingdom.

Go on, speed away and find her said a voice in his head but the dark matter which perpetually threatened him took hold of his inner gravity once again and he continued with his relentless quest for destruction; he slotted the red memory stick into his computer and set about solving the issue of the extra memory use.

The original mental state report had been corrupted by his software, because he was on an oldish Windows system which reduced part of every new document to a meaningless jumble of hieroglyphics streaming down the page in a monstrous DNA sequence. That's what had happened with this document too, so he'd failed to notice an island of sense at the very bottom of the sequence. He'd missed it until now – a second mental assessment at the psychiatric unit, which involved Pryderi to a certain degree but which now introduced another person. His mother, Rhiannon.

Following the same formula as the first assessment, Rhiannon's document also logged her appearance, noting that she was reasonably tidy in a worn but clean horse-riding outfit which included jodhpurs and tall riding boots. She had arrived at the door of the unit leading a seventeen-hand stallion, and she had stood looking at the building as if it were a newly landed spaceship. The horse had stomped and neighed; these sounds had alerted Pryderi, who immediately went to the entrance to find her. They had embraced each other for a long time, rocking from side to side, and both had wept. Then, Pryderi had led her by the hand into the unit, leaving the horse tied to railings outside (it was taken away to local stables later that day).

Rhiannon and Pryderi had sat in the same wordless state, moving away from people whenever they approached, seeking only each other's company, either in the quiet room or in the garden; often they could be seen sitting on the marble lip of the ornamental fountain holding hands, listening to the gurgle of the water but saying nothing – as if both had signed a vow of silence. One staff member claimed that Rhiannon had said a single sentence as she held Pryderi that first time outside the entrance: something like *Oh God Pryderi, what are you doing in here?*

The theory among staff was that Rhiannon, whoever she was, had decided not to talk as an instinctive act of solidarity; the link between the two was unknown, but it was clear that they were either related or very close friends. In this state they had stayed glued together as the days drifted by, in retreat from the world.

They weren't unco-operative, but neither did

they communicate with the staff. The need to find a solution became urgent, according to the assessment notes, or both of them would be there for ever.

No one came to see them, and so the months drifted by. Early winter arrived and with it came the equinox storms. Pryderi and Rhiannon could be seen at the window of the quiet room, watching lightning fork over Wales, listening to the storm winds. One night a terrible clap of thunder seemed to affect them more than the others; they took fright and tried to escape from the unit. One of the patients claimed that a gun had been fired, though there was no evidence for that. But the next day, for their own safety, the pair were sectioned and the outside world became a place beyond walls for them both. From that day on they were sealed away in a glass cabinet.

Lou closed the document and tried to breathe slowly and deeply, the way they'd taught him on the anger management course. But the dark matter within him massed again and sent his hand towards the mouse. In a series of slow, deliberate movements he highlighted the document and deleted it, leaving the memory stick completely blank. Then he emptied the recycle bin to make absolutely sure that everything was gone and detached the stick from its hole in the tower unit. It tinkled against the porcelain when he tossed it into the fruit bowl.

That was it. He'd expressed himself in the only way he knew how, and the story was dead. He'd go to see the prof tomorrow and tell him some sob story, kill the whole damn thing stone dead. He might even resign. The Big M story had been consigned to a few footnotes in history. Whatever his motives, which were complex and irritating, he'd extracted revenge on Feeney and academia in general. Perhaps he would have to explain his actions. As for now, he'd go home to look after his wife and baby child. That's what society expected of him.

But when he arrived home she was gone. There was a note on the table, but it didn't bring him any joy. Because Llwyd McNamara's world was really breaking up now, and he was in deep trouble. He knew it, too.

VI

An eerie, pregnant silence met Lou when he arrived home. As soon as he opened the door he suspected that something had changed. Old intuitions kicked in – those subliminal instincts which come into play when we suspect that someone is looking at us from behind, or following us.

Now, standing in the hallway with its pattern of blood-and-sand-coloured tiles, he sensed that there was no one there – the building had a cold, empty feel. He called her name, quietly then loudly and insistently, but there was no response. He bounded up the stairs and poked his head round all the doors, but every room held the same sarcophagal silence. Upstairs was like a morgue without a body; the newly painted nursery jangled his nerves and he experienced a few moments of panic and sickness.

Wondering what to do next, he wound up the Birdytweet mobile hanging over the empty cot and watched seven little plastic birds circle the empty nest below, moving their wings jerkily and twittering a mechanical dirge as their little beaks opened and closed. Lou was overwhelmed by sadness, and he was forced to sit down for a while. It was a tristesse which started with his own birth and then passed like a shadow over the tragi-comic minutiae of his life, before passing over the life of his unborn child also, through every rainy day and every small reversal, until the time came, many years in the future, when the child would wind up his own plastic birds in his own newly decorated nursery and feel the same timeswept sadness.

What if Catrin was ill? More importantly, was he culpable if she'd lost the baby? Had he been attentive enough? Had he actually cared enough, had he really meant it when he'd promised to be a good father? Or had the last few months indicated to Catrin that his own agenda was far more important to him than fatherhood? What had he been doing while her belly swelled and her mind fronded delicately in the luxuriant gardens of impending motherhood? Had he been there for her, his parental promise shining in his eyes? No, probably not. His distraction may have been evident as he pursued the Big M story; maybe they'd disengaged and drifted apart from each other, she retreating to her friends and her books, he to his corrosive microworld inside the memory sticks.

Lou had a resigned air when he walked downstairs, because by then he felt sure that Catrin had gone, possibly for ever, in the way that women sometimes make monumental decisions at crucial times, and then stick to them unerringly. Downstairs looked the same as it always had since Catrin became pregnant. She'd become obsessively clean and tidy; the work-tops gleamed and the flowers beamed as usual in their vases, but there was one stark difference: Catrin's absence was almost a physical presence. The lower rooms sat there in dumb resignation, as if they were three hostages who had been gagged, blindfolded and trussed up by burglars. But as he turned away from the sitting room he noticed an envelope leaning against the fruit bowl on their newly bought Ikea coffee table, with a scrawl on it. Closer up he saw his name – the Welsh version, Llwyd – underlined decisively. It had all the appearance of a Dear John letter, and when he opened it he saw that it contained two items. The first was a simple home-made card showing the view from his college window (when had she taken that?) with a short message inside:

Gone away to the coast for a few days to think things over. It's been like living with a stranger recently, a stranger I don't like very much. What happened, Llwyd? Did I do something? Why have you changed so much since I fell pregnant? I need to sort my head out. Catrin.

PS The Vice-Chancellor delivered this on his way to the airport, said he'd been very busy and he'd forgotten about it. He also said he hadn't seen you for a while and he seemed worried about you.

The object she referred to had fallen onto the glass surface of the table when he removed the card. It whirred and tinkled, giving off a sparkling rotating light before wobbling to a standstill. Lou was fascinated by it and he toyed with it for a while, spinning it around in the palm of his left hand. It was just like the others, holding its silvery innards in a pretty plastic jacket; the only difference was that this one was light blue in colour. Once again he had the feeling that he was being toyed with. So the vice-chancellor *had just happened* to drop it by on his way to the airport. A likely story. And there was another thing which struck him: the first memory stick had come to him via a minor academic; the second had come from a professor, and this last one had come from the top dog himself. Lou was puzzled. Why would academia want to play silly buggers with a lowly pawn like him? Perhaps it was all a huge coincidence. Perhaps he was imagining things.

Catrin was already forgotten by the time he'd jabbed the blue memory stick into his laptop in the study.

He watched the tail-light flashing its firefly signal; and since he had no mouse now he used his finger-pad to open its contents. It seemed to hold a number of documents, but again they were being corrupted by his software and he encountered a wasteland of meaningless symbols and signs before he found anything comprehensible. Two of the documents were virtually indecipherable, but a few subtle clues led him to the conclusion that they contained all the information which had come to him on the green and red sticks, but which he'd killed off on his computer at the college. He blanched. All that vitriol he'd shown had been a complete waste of emotion. Pissing in the wind. He'd spent an enormous amount of malign energy and sadistic forethought to no purpose. All the information had survived on this stick – and on many others, probably. He'd been outwitted, and once again the feeling came over him that he was being used. Powerful forces were at play, and he was being manipulated. Worse still, he had no idea who was playing cat and mouse with him, or why he was being kicked like an under-inflated ball from one end of the academic field to the other.

According to the blue memory stick, Big M and Ziggy had made occasional visits to the leper huts by the hospital to visit Rhiannon and Pryderi, but both inmates had become locked in some sort of mother-son complex, or a wordless relationship like Olaf the Peacock and this mute thrall-woman. By now they were living in their own submersible bubble, a diving chamber floating way below everyone else in a lagoon of silence. And because of official protocol the two on the outside weren't allowed to know any details of their condition. Big M and Ziggy could only assume that an old trauma had been reactivated. Although facts were in short supply, they knew that Pryderi had been separated from his mother when he was very young, and that neither of them had been able to talk about the issue at any time in their lives. Perhaps the gunshot at Hotel Corvo had lit a slow fuse, or maybe the incident with the badger had acted as a catalyst. There was something about the smell of a badger, pungent and porcine, which came straight from prehistory; it had a musk-like ability to arouse primal fears and desires.

However, after months of getting nowhere, Big M and Ziggy had visited less and less frequently, since the drive over to the unit took a tankful of petrol and they were running short of ready money – Pryderi was the keeper of the purse, and he'd kept all the spondoolicks in his back pocket. After many months like this the situation had become desperate and the duo on the outside were forced to dream up an alternative plan. They had to act quickly in the end because a new and more pressing problem arrived to drive them on. This problem was well documented in the blue memory stick. Having trawled through it, and having spent a lot of time knocking out the corrupt matter and deciphering its absurd jumble, Lou was able to recover and isolate a new segment at the end which shone a new light on this period in Big M's history. It was in the form of a diary, probably an extract from a much larger document. The diarist was obviously Ziggy, and her starting point was the very end of autumn that year, when she was staying at the boarded-up Hotel Corvo with Big M, just the two of them thrown together now. It had been a difficult time, evidently. Ziggy had really missed her husband, and she was also worried that she might succumb to Big M's legendary charms. She confided in her diary that a storm was brewing, in more ways than one. Two erotically charged, sex-starved people benighted in a ghostly hotel with nobody else in sight was a recipe for disaster. The diary entries began on her thirtieth birthday.

> October 21 – Happy birthday (not) to me. What a way to celebrate – I already hate being thirty, lines around my eyes and nothing to wear on my first date with Mr Gravity. Checked for stretch marks & cellulite etc, OK for now but the only way is down. Massive depression, not helped by the fact that P won't talk to me, squats in his hut with the other maniacs and holds hands with his mum, what does that mean? Where am I in all this? Lost in wild Wales with

no company, not much food, and as of yesterday no electricity either. Cut off. M gave me a kiss and promised to cook me a smurfday dinner. Told him I needed a big party with loads of people but he waved at the outside world and said *you find me some people and I'll organise the party*. So I went into a bad place, got grumpy with him. He tried to cuddle up but I wasn't having any of that, dirty sod, I know where he's been.

October 21 evening – Fair play, he made a real effort. Bless. I was sitting upstairs in my room, looking out over the sea, feeling low – can't concentrate on anything, this last year always on my mind. Hotel Corvo boarded up, everyone gone. All those good times we had, hotel heaving, party every night. Sea wild today, crashing on the cliffs in huge white waves and throwing foam and spray all over the lower fields. I could hear the roar, awesome. Decided to make an effort for my birthday in the afternoon so got dolled up, went downstairs and suggested a run over to the psychiatric unit. Big mistake, P wouldn't even see me so I walked out feeling really shitty and we came back in silence, M trying to be supportive and loyal as usual, which only made things worse. Running out of fags so feeling very tense. Worst birthday of my life. Then, when I was back in my room wondering if things could get any worse, a knock on the door and ta-rah! M was there with a trolley – he was wearing his chef's hat with the blue band, big meal laid out in no time, really good of him. Delish food with two magnums of Moet & Chandon – trying to get me pissed by the look of things. Sitting there like a couple of lovebirds, he went off on one about birthdays and star signs; he's into astrology (or pretends to be). Said he'd cooked the perfect meal for a Libran like me, romantic and idealistic, and he was generally mega charming. Found myself flirting back at him but after a while I started to feel drunk & a bit paranoid because I know from bitter experience that Librans are gullible and easy to fool so I went all quiet and broody. What's up says M, did I say something? No, just feeling a bit vulnerable I say. He puts his paw on mine, looks at me with those big blue eyes of his and I get suspicious, pull my hand away and ask him if he's trying it on. God no, he says. I could trust him completely, blah-de-blah, usual ape-talk. I say I know about the other women.

Ach, says M, they were just a bit of fun. Rhiannon knew all about them, she also knew that they meant nothing to him. So I reply *typical male, double standards*, and he just laughs, it's just a joke to him.

You won't be doing any sex god stuff with me I can tell you now, says I, you can keep your mitts to yourself and no mistaking. Then I get hiccups and he laughs even more. We end up talking about star signs, how desperate can you get, but I wanted to start a row so I could put some space between us. Turns out he's Taurus and he says he's typical – practical, reliable, stubborn, laid back, comfort-loving, stable, tenacious, strong, successful.

But don't worry luv, Taureans and Librans aren't compatible, he says all nonchalant, sitting back with that annoying habit he has of putting his feet up on the nearest chair after a meal. What I don't tell him is that Libran girls and Taurean males get on just great between the sheets, good sexual chemistry, but after that there's nothing, not enough to keep them together for a day. But I don't say that in case he gets funny ideas. Actually, says M all innocent, Librans and Taureans are supposed to have terrific sexual rapport. Both born under Venus, lots of passion.

That was enough for me, I grabbed one of the bottles and went upstairs without another word, locked the door and got stonking pissed. Woke up in the night, face down on the bed in a puddle of champagne.

October 24 – He's not there in the morning, returns at noon with his rod and a bag over his shoulder. He's all over me when we meet on the stairs, sorry this sorry that, head down like a naughty boy. He says *for God's sake Ziggy, I absolutely promise you that I wasn't trying to take advantage last night. Just fooling around, you know me. And you've got to admit you were pretty flirty yourself.*

I was pissed, keep well away from me you animal, says I.

He holds his head in his hands and says *no no no* in a quiet voice, sounds desperate. You've got it all wrong, he moans, and he looks at me imploringly.

But I leave him on the stairs and tell him to keep away. Men are all the same, walking pricks. Anyway, I say as I walk away, we've got to make some money quick or we'll starve to death. Got any bright ideas? I slam the door and lock it. Hopefully he's got the message now.

October 28 – I've spent a few days trying to work out how we could make some dosh. Made a list of our strengths and weaknesses and it's obvious that M's rugby fame is our biggest asset. Why not market a new-style rugby boot with his name on it? We could get a grant. Will suggest it to him tomorrow.

October 29 – The rugby boot idea went down like a lead balloon. He says he's been out of the game too long, people want a happening person, someone on the scene right now. Spent the day in my room putting together a business plan. I'm sure it's a possibility. What else can we do in a place with no people, no jobs? Heard him rattling on my door, saying *let me in Ziggy, I need to talk to you* but I ignore him, let him stew. *Are you all right in there*, he asks in his best voice but I stay by the window, smoking. Down to my last 100 fags now, will have to do something soon. Maybe leave without him?

October 30 – Breakthrough! I tell him about my plan to go it alone and he comes over all soft and concerned, says he can't let me go away on my own, he's promised Pryderi he'll look after me etc. etc. I beg him to consider my plan.

But Ziggy, he says, who'll design these boots, how do we make them? What about finance?

Listen, I say to him, I've got it all sorted. We've got to leave Wales, no jobs here. Never has been much to do around here except be Welsh, been like that since the Ice Age. We've got to go back to England for a while, they love fiddling about with their little businesses, it's in their blood. Something to do with neat Saxon compounds, goats in tidy little pens, yeoman values, puritan prosperity. We'll get a grant easy peasy, set up shop on one of those interminable industrial estates with bleeping lorries and pallets stacked up like bodies at Belsen. Scenes from a zombie movie every dinnertime, dead-eyed people wandering about looking for flesh.

I say to him – you design the shoes and I'll market them, we're onto a winner. Besides, I'm running out of fags.

Can't argue with that, says M.

Anyway, I wouldn't be able to hold out much longer, says I.

Meaning?

Those deadly charms of yours would get to me eventually. I can feel myself weakening.

He comes over and gives me a hug. Brotherly, keeps his pelvis well away from me.

Ziggy, you're a crazy woman, he says. Any other time I'd be running after you with a club, you're gorgeous, but I'm a nice guy, really. Rhiannon and me, we're for life now. And you and Pryderi will be together soon, I just know it somehow. He'll come out of it one day a happier man, trust me. We'll have a big party at Hotel Corvo, we'll open those windows and give the place a lick of paint. Seven bars humming every night, good times again. Trust me? He steps away and holds me at arm's length.

He's smiling like he's everyone's best friend. Those flecks in his eyes seem extra lovely, I feel a tug.

Yes, I say. I trust you. Now let's get the Bentley and go. An hour later we're on the road with two cases in the back and just enough petrol – maybe – to get us over the border. Besides, I say to his left profile, it would be nice to see some real living people again.

Even if they're English?

Even if they're Martian, I reply.

I like the open road, top down. Don't care if I never see Hotel Corvo ever again. I know we'll go back to get P and R when they're in better shape. Sometimes people need to be left alone to sort things out. Mental illness builds a wall around you, like you're an obscene statue with huge naughty bits, people want to hide you from children and *Daily Express* types.

M holds my hand for a bit and I know it's all right now, he's not on heat. He's a real gent really, gone up in my estimation. I squeeze his hand and tell him so. I like the way a web of little white lines spreads around the corners of his eyes, slicing up the sunburn. I like the smell of him too, solid and warm. He was in blue denim today with strap leather boots. Still in good shape, one of those men who keep their looks till they're old I'd say. He's like a brother to me now, I feel safe. What a relief. The Bentley hums along country roads, air coming in bands of warm and cool. Green and brown smells, cattle vapours, huge oaks crouched like trolls by the roadside, ready to pick us up and swallow us.

November 1 – We arrived late in the evening at a border town, some thirty miles into England. Petrol low and we failed to find anywhere to stay, so he put the top up and we slept under rugs in the car, somewhere quiet by the river. We were dropping off, me on the back seat, him in the front, when a copper arrived to annoy us, shining his torch through the windows. Asked us what we were doing. Told him we'd heard the streets were paved with gold, wanted to get rich quick, seen *The Apprentice* and knew it was a doddle in England, everyone a millionaire. He got suspicious and asked us if we were Welsh, suggested we buggered off back home. We managed to pacify him, fortunately the cop was a rugger fan and when he found out who Big M was the two of them were off talking about rugby until I got testy.

November 2 – Managed to find a cheap B&B but we had to sell the Bentley, nearly broke M's heart. Never actually seen him in that state before, he's usually so even tempered & accepts everything that comes, in that cool way of his. Bentley another matter, I thought he was going to cry. It wasn't the value of the motor or the kudos of driving it, he said. He just loved its sheer good looks and its classiness. Like his footwear and his clothes, M likes top stuff. Says he was born like that, regal tastes.

November 3 – M in a funk, completely thrown by the Bentley sell-off. Moping around, so I went out and bought a couple of sketch pads and some colouring pens, told him to draw. Mournful looks all round. But Ziggy, he says, we've lost everything now. I can cope without any people, he says, I can cope without a home, but I can't cope without any *style* in my life.

Well get weaving, I says. Design some great shoes, set the rugby world on fire. You've got the golden touch, everything you've done has star quality.

Ziggy, do you really mean that? he asks.

Of course I really mean it you plonker, look at your track record, I says. Great rugby player, brilliant cook, all round nice guy and great friend...

Can it be that this guy has no confidence in himself, under all that bravado?

Bloody men, they always manage to surprise me. Don't try to tell me there's a sensitive little soul lurking beneath the surface. National hero, or is he just a little wuss?

November 5 – Really busy week, setting up the business. For now the boots are called Big M's. Enterprise Agency have agreed to give us a free home for a year and free advertising for a month, then it's up to us. M will have to get some more dosh from P, then off we go. M's designs look great to me, but what do I know about rugby boots?

He's asked me to go back to the huts with him to see P and R, get some money. Don't know if I can face P, all this action has taken my mind off things and I've enjoyed it all. M has been great fun, his enthusiasm infectious. Initial eBay run of 150 boots – with a signed picture of M taken on the day Wales beat Ireland at Dublin – have sold within a few days, so things look good.

November 12 – Manufacturing unit on the industrial estate starts full-time work with an initial staff of 12, using imported Sami reindeer leather, with his signature in gold, final product nicely packaged and sold at sports outlets in Britain's main cities as well as on the web. Orders very encouraging. Bank not so impressed and wants £10,000 injected into our account asap, so we're off back to Wales tomorrow. Need to see P anyway.

November 13 – Drove back to Wales in a hired saloon, M grumbled and made me drive. We got to the psychiatric unit at dinner time and had to wait in the foyer till they'd finished. Both of them came out to see us, hugs all round and a bit of hope I think; at least their eyes were alive, looking at us sadly but clearly. M managed to get a wad of cash off P, said it was urgent or Hotel Corvo would go into repossess and we'd all have to move to a council house, that's if we could get one. We promised we'd be back soon to take them home. Tried to give them some hope.

November 20 – Things going well, cash flow has increased. M's designs are wowing everyone;

one of the Welsh stars has promised to wear a pair for this year's internationals so it's all going in the right direction.

December 1 – Bad news, very bad. Couple of hoods walked into the office today, waved a gun and frightened us all. Shades, expensive suits, could have been the same mob as the Hotel Corvo outfit. Told us we'd outstayed our welcome, the Welsh weren't welcome on their manor. Gave us a week to sell up and move on. M just sat there in his chair without saying a word. Wasn't much point really with a Smith and Wesson stuffed up one of his lugholes.

Why can't they leave us alone Ziggy, he says afterwards. Is it me or something?

We sit around, trying to decide what to do. If it's the same mob following us around, playing cat and mouse with us, we're in deep shit. They won't mess around. Shallow grave in the woods, farewell cruel world.

Lou unscrambled the final part, which had been added as a coda by someone else. Faced with an execution-style death, Ziggy and Big M had no option but to cut and run. This time it was Ziggy who was heartbroken; seeing all her hard work go down the drain was too much. They lost almost everything – the bank took the business and left them with a grand to get home. Even Lou was moved by their final plight: left with nothing but their clothes and a few belongings, they'd had to buy old charity-shop rucksacks and hitch to the border. From there they got back to Hotel Corvo by attaching themselves to a small travelling fairground which was moving westwards; the journey must have taken many weeks. Apparently Big M had earned his keep by fooling around in a clown's outfit, complete with red nose, revolving bow tie, water-squirting flower and floppy outsize shoes. Even in adversity he'd managed to hold on to his unusual footwear. Lou had a vision of a small convoy of wagons, trailers and caravans travelling slowly under a huge western sky; he saw the big top on a village green somewhere, ringed by the yellow grasses of winter; and finally he saw Big M's clown-face captured in a swag of multi-coloured bulbs: his hair shining purple, his hands green, his feet mauve.

When they got to their home patch in the western region the audiences had faltered and then dwindled to none, as people began to recognise Ziggy and Big M; the old curse had returned. It seems that the two of them had left the troupe rather emotionally because they'd grown to like their new friends, and had fitted in well.

They completed their return to Hotel Corvo in a battered taxi, after calling at a supermarket to stock up on tinned goods and essentials, and then at a farmers' co-operative to get some seeds and grain. They knew that life at Hotel Corvo would be difficult and bare as they waited for Pryderi and Rhiannon to recover; Big M planned to grow all their own food, since they would have to be self-sufficient and resourceful. A hard winter lay ahead, the two of them living alone on the wild, remote cliffs of Dyfed.

Lou heard the doorbell ring and a huge adrenalin rush set his heart racing. Was that Catrin, returning? But no, she had a key of course. The police? *Would you like to sit down Mr McNamara, we have some news for you...*

He took the stairs in a rapid shuffle and opened the door to a young female face. It took quite a few seconds for him to recognise their Polish cleaner, Anka. He waved her in, but she immediately flustered and started to retreat. What could be the matter with the silly bitch? She stammered something in Polish and fluttered her hands apologetically, adding a confused sentence in broken English: *I come again tomorrow maybe if Mrs McNamara here...*

Then he remembered that he'd goosed her neat little bottom when he'd passed her in the hallway on his way to work the last time they'd met. Stupid girl, didn't it go with the job?

He closed the door on her and returned upstairs, where he retrieved the memory stick and put the computer to sleep. After that he made himself a sandwich and sat in the kitchen, trying to form a plan. He'd have to do something about Catrin, or their relationship would be buggered for ever. That's if it wasn't already. And if she had genuinely disappeared the police might wonder why he hadn't tried to find her. But where was she? West Wales, probably – her note had mentioned the coast, and her sister had a caravan not so far from Hotel Corvo. He'd mentioned the hotel to her so many times that she'd been fascinated by it. It seemed that fate was about to lead him back there again. Twice the place had drawn him in and enthralled him. Now, for a third time, he would have to return there to finish the matter.

He considered the word *fate*, and dismissed it. No, he was sure by now that he was being pulled into a man-made web. He would have to find out who was responsible. He put his plate in the sink, without washing it, and got ready to go.

VII

Driving westwards in his BMW, Lou broke down. He hoped it wasn't a sign. By the time he'd been lugged home on a breakdown lorry it was late, so he bedded down for the night. A full moon illuminated the nursery as he passed it, and the empty, silver-washed room held an unearthly stillness which unnerved him. He slept badly.

Wales was basking under a warm autumnal sun when he recovered his car from the garage the following day. The sky was blue with a train of clouds on the horizon ahead of him as he drove; he couldn't help but think of the blue memory stick in his pocket, which like the other memory sticks held a huge empty world within it, vast tracts of uninhabited land dotted with small bands of men on horseback and occasional plumes of woodsmoke, passed over silently by flocculent clouds, beautiful and mysterious. Once again he was struck by a vision of worlds within worlds, a triple mandala in which he saw a big blue Earth as seen from space, then his small blue car on its revolving surface, then a tiny blue capsule within the moving vehicle. Ever diminishing circles. Three dimensions, three whorls of related matter. Then his mind drifted to an early Celtic speciality, the triple death – ritual murder by wounding, strangulation and drowning. One after the other. You'd be completely dead after that. He felt his neck and imagined a stranger's hand gripping his hair, pulling his head back, preparing to kill him. Lou feared death squeamishly, terribly.

All around him Wales was changing hue; a slow colour wash was bleaching out the sharpness in the reds, greens and blues. Mellow and slightly melancholic, a series of duns and browns came into view; the landscape became a rag rug lying in rucked buffs and ochres. The wheatfields swayed towards him and then swayed away from him drunkenly in various fawny shades. On both sides of the road, in fields dipping and slanting under huge rolling cumuli, he could see kine chewing the cud contentedly or sheep, plump and shorn, moving slowly along as they enjoyed a brief siesta before their annual lamb-bearing cycle started all over again. The country around him was huge and beautiful, yet Lou felt no joy in looking at it. He was a town mouse by nature, more at home in the brick conduits of man-made structures, which was probably why he preferred the fairy world of the memory sticks to the Olympian vistas now opening up in front of him. He struggled to cope with the scale of the natural world, its monumental cycles of birth and death, its absolute indifference to him. As Catrin had noticed, Lou was one for scuttling into the countryside for brief circular walks recommended by the Sunday supplements, and after buying an expensive pair of walking shoes – which he'd use maybe half a dozen times in his life – he liked to dart back home again, feeling virtuous.

This time, feeling not in the least bit virtuous,

he was heading for Hotel Corvo again, and for no particular reason he was driving too fast: screeching through the bends, rocking along the straights. Was he trying to add a bit of drama to his search for Catrin? Or merely being childishly *Top Gear* about his journey? Maybe the contents of his mind were responsible: he was dwelling once again on his reasons for trying to obliterate all the alternative versions of the Big M story before he wrote his own. He was already aware that university arts faculties were small Petri colonies, at best polemical, at worst parasitic; a minor national poet or novelist might occasionally feel the grazing snout of a collegiate shark touching his skin, while a famous figure such as R.S. Thomas, cast into the Well of Knowledge, would have his body stripped to the bone within minutes in a piranha frenzy. His own college had become a capitalist sausage machine, squeezing as many plump little middle-class kids as it could through the machinery and then making extravagant claims on the packaging when they flopped out on the other side. Little more than a rubber stamp, really

– the kids largely taught themselves online and emerged three years later, thirty grand in debt and feeling mugged. As his own professor had admitted at a party, three sheets to the wind, modern learning was all fur coat and no knickers. But who wanted to read fusty old books about the past when you could get all you needed in seconds via Wiki?

On the other hand, Lou wanted to establish a reputation, and a good book bearing his name would set him on the road to success. That meant elbowing the competition aside and shouting loudest. That was the main reason, probably, for his ungentlemanly conduct with the memory sticks. But he'd been upstaged by someone else, and he wanted to know who it was. Maybe that was the reason for his urge to reach Catrin as quickly as possible. It certainly wasn't a need to find her. On the contrary, he feared seeing her again because he knew it would mean some sort of showdown.

Anger erupted inside him. Failure, failure, everything he touched had been a failure. Why had he sold his soul to the education factory? Damn and double damn. In Mitteleuropa one could still see vestiges of the Enlightenment – excited young faces, fresh and hopeful, picking lush fruits from the Tree of Knowledge in a celebration of beautiful intellects; but here in Britain the students had been herded into a side-chapel and conned into buying indulgences and expensive relics from the pardoner's seventh cousin removed. Meanwhile, Lou had jumped onto every gravy train passing but had missed the boat, the main boat, the big silvery boat which took a select few to literature's island of apples. Hunched in his car – a small and transient object like himself – he saw clearly now that his time had come in an instant and had gone in an instant, like a moment in the life of a circus – his pitiable existence little more than a single subtle foolery by the clown; he had blinked and missed it.

Tired but no longer angry, looking drawn and defeated, Lou finally arrived at Hotel Corvo and sat for a while, listening to a white silky silence being embroidered by the songbirds. In the distance he could hear the faint boom of the sea when it struck the cliffs. A flight of noisy jackdaws swirled and left the building, which had closed yet again and was boarded up. It looked as derelict and abandoned as his memory sticks had recorded. He looked up at the missing sign and it was still missing; the only changes he could spot were graffiti scrawls left by local louts who'd wandered there on drug and drink expeditions, their modern initiation rites. The scene held one unexpected item though, a large pantechnicon with a satellite dish on its roof; two rampant red dragons emblazoned on its flanks were overwritten with the name of a well-known Welsh television company, *Ystrad Fflur.* Locked up and left to its own devices, it squatted on the potholed tarmac like a huge blind beetle waiting to be eaten from within by another insect's parasitic eggs, already hatching in its bowels. Above it, the sky was patterned with vapour trails. Which poet had compared those high, silent jets to small perfect gods on the run from adoration? Lou couldn't remember.

He walked around the abandoned hotel, peeping through holes in its boarded-up windows; then he stared at the rusty brackets which had once held the Hotel Corvo sign, when the place was in its pomp – before that fateful gunshot. Nostalgia crept through him and he longed to be there once again when he was a young pimply thing, with the world at his feet, every girlie in the land available to him. He threw individual chippings at the bracket lamps on either side of the main door and eventually smashed the thick glass panel around one of them. He squatted among the weeds and pieced together the fragments, which spelled the name of an old brewing company long since swallowed up by another. He realised how pathetic he was being, and retreated to the car. He'd better be going, though the thought of coming face to face with Catrin again sent an acidic jolt through him. So he wasted some more time by going up to the lorry and examining it at close quarters. He tested the doors and kicked the tyres, but the vehicle ignored him patiently. Turning away from it, he looked at the landscape below him, which featured a series of small brackened fields slipping away towards the cliffs. Looking southwards he could see the coastal path weaving its way along the lip of the land before dipping away out of sight. He knew from his adolescence that the pathway left the cliff at that point and moved slightly inland, skirting a plateau of small fields which sheltered in the lee of a clifftop ridge; he remembered a beautiful enclosure or glade surrounded by scrub oak and bracken, overlooking the Dyfed landscape with its blanket of tiny fields stretching into the distance. Staring towards this plateau, which was just out of vision, he caught sight of someone, so he decided to walk towards the figure. The man or woman stood gaunt and unmoving, leaning towards the sea, with only the head and torso visible. One of the film crew, maybe, thought Lou as he ambled towards it. But as he entered the plateau he realised that the figure was a scarecrow, standing slightly awry on its one good leg. Walking up to it through the crop, he was struck by a similarity between the scarecrow and himself. The likeness was created by the scarecrow's clothes, which might have come from his own wardrobe. In fact, the closer he examined them the surer he was that they had indeed come from his clothes cupboard back home. The hat, too, was surely one of his – a sou'wester he'd worn on his stag night; and to complete the scarecrow's air of idiocy someone had slung a revolting green rucksack on its back – a rucksack remarkably like one of his own. Lou's face flushed with embarrassment and anger. Was someone taking the piss? And who was the clothes thief? The answer had to be Catrin. Was she in on the conspiracy too? Lou thrust his hands in his pockets and started to sulk. He was standing in a small triangular field of corn, ready to be harvested by the look of it, and the scarecrow was planted right in the middle of it. It bore a comical, triumphant air, as if a grimacing clown, in tripping over his ridiculous shoes in the centre of a ring, had managed to convey in the moment of falling an ironic message – *I told you this was going to happen.*

Lou walked onwards through the corn, not caring how much damage he did, and entered a second field which was bigger than the first, a thorax which continued the triangular shape of the plateau. Again, there was a scarecrow in the middle, which also bore a resemblance to Lou; this one wore a suspiciously Lou-like coat and another ridiculous bag was slung over its shoulder, this one red. Lou carried on towards another field, in a high dudgeon by now, but then he changed course and slunk towards the blackthorn hedge on the landward side when he saw a group of people at the far end of the third field.

Moving towards them with cat-like movements in the shade of the stooped bushes, which had been bent into old men by the sea winds, he began to pick up snatches of conversation. *Are you ready now... the sound boom's in vision... can you move right into the corn please, it looks better...*

He got as close as he could without being spotted, and surveyed the scene. By now a tall man and a young woman were standing up to their thighs in the golden crop, he with a hand around her waist, guiding her into the corn. He was a big man, broad and powerful, dressed in blue denim. The woman was Catrin, dressed in a fresh white muslin dress, and she looked radiant. Lou watched them with a cold, steely hatred. Between his lair and the two subjects stood a camera crew, in a small clearing cut ready for them in the corn, and they were about to start filming.

'Right, ready when you are,' said a voice from somewhere. Then the man in denim began to talk to camera.

We came back here after being chased out of England yet again...

'Cut!' said the disembodied voice. 'Can we leave out the England bit please, no point in being antagonistic, they'll only switch off...'

The man in denim thought about this for a few seconds, adjusted his stance, and then started again.

We came here to run Hotel Corvo, but we had to close the hotel and find other work. There were four involved in the business originally, but two had to have psychiatric care because they couldn't cope with failure, and to be honest the general state of the world around us also had a negative effect. After trying a number of ideas we decided to set up our own sustainable smallholding, here on this farm by the sea. Three years down the line we're all feeling much happier, more in control of our lives, and the two who spent time in care are almost ready to rejoin us, because this venture has given them hope. A number of other people have joined us and we're a small commune now – meet our newest member, Catrin McNamara, who got fed up with worsening social conditions and joined us only this week. She wants a better, more natural life for her unborn baby...

He turned to her affectionately, and continued:

The great capitalist dream is ending, as it was bound to. Nothing is for ever, and though we had a good time in the material world we realised that we had to become self-sufficient as the West's dependence on oil and consumerism hit the buffers. It's not all sweetness and light here, there are constant worries over health care and food, and we have to defend ourselves against maurading gangs, but we're a lot happier as a small co-operative. We feel that we all count in one way or another, we can see democracy in action every day. We all have something to contribute, and we live in a very beautiful place – which is good for the soul...

Here he swept a hand towards the amazing view below them.

Lou could take no more, so he crept away in the shadow of the hedge, until he was safely out of sight. Then he careered across the fields, uprooting the scarecrows and grabbing wildly at corn stalks, flinging them into the air around him. After he'd finished his mad dervish dance through the cornfields he went to the car and sat in it for a while, planning his next move whilst removing ears of corn from his clothing. He realised that he was in a near-psychotic state by now, but he didn't care. The adrenalin rush he'd got from his mini-rampage had merely fuelled another onslaught, which would come later. He knew now what it was like to be part of a riot. He'd enjoyed the power surge, the sub-erotic pleasure of wanton destruction. Smashing things was fun, and he'd be back later to enjoy some more. University researcher? Sod it, this was much more enjoyable. Smiling grimly to himself, he started the car and headed for the nearest town to get some grub. He'd be back later, under the cover of darkness, and he knew what he was going to do.

It was close to midnight, the witching hour, when Lou – still trying to digest a greasy burger meal – fired up his saloon in the Hotel Corvo car park.

The film crew had gone and he'd sat there alone, watching the last few jackdaws settling down for the night, a noisy gang jostling among the chimneys high above him. The place was theirs now; it was unlikely to open again as a going concern. Such places were disappearing all along Britain's coastline, wayside markers for a lost way of life. Nowadays, inside their expensive little huts, the people of Britain watched placebo TV, swigged cheap supermarket beer or boxed wine, and obediently forgot how to commune with either nature or their fellow humans. The ersatz world screened to them daily presented a nostalgic dream of a country which existed only in miniature now, a ship in a bottle.

Lou revved up the car and headed for a cart track he'd spotted earlier, which would take him towards the sleeping cornfields and their busy mice. After wrenching the gate off its hinges in the glare of the headlights he entered the first field and started his rampage. Startled rabbits shot through the hedges as he mowed his way through the corn in anarchic loops, his headlights sweeping across the countryside and out to sea in crazy, spyrographic patterns. Grasping the steering wheel at arm's length, Lou screamed and shouted as he went, bouncing and rattling in his seat, destroying the crop in a mad orgy of destruction. Even then, as his vengeance peaked, his mind was elsewhere – inside one of the memory sticks, racing up and down the silvery circuits, wiping out the contents, erasing all the memories, mowing down Big M and ejecting him into the dustbin of history. As he entered the second field he decided to try his hand at a crop circle which would spell his name, but he gave up after a while because it was too difficult. An owl, white and spectral, crossed his headlights. Bats flitted out of his way. And then, as his pillage in the second field reached a crescendo and he prepared to enter the third, the whole world jarred to a halt. He hadn't seen it until the last moment – a rock lying in its own little glade within the corn, a large granite mouse crouched in the crop. He'd driven straight onto its back and the car had become stranded on it, its mechanical belly hooked by two large granite ears which held it firmly. The wheels continued to whirr in a high-pitched scream, and then the engine stalled. Lou sat there in his poleaxed saddle, resting on the back of a fossilised Precambrian supermouse. Then a hairy hand wrenched open the door nearest to him and pulled him out of the vehicle. After that, the world went black.

He was out for a long time, and they were beginning to worry. But eventually he stirred, and after the preliminaries to consciousness he came to. He looked around him but failed to make any connection with his new surroundings. He was in a small room with uneven walls, painted in a bright yellow ochre. A few candles shimmered here and there, their flames wafted occasionally by a draught, or perhaps by someone moving. The air smelt of mud and straw; primitive, elemental. He struggled to focus, and on turning his head he saw two human faces looking at him, waiting for him to recover.

'Sorry about that Llwyd,' said a faraway voice. 'We got a bit carried away, but you were destroying our food for the winter.'

He spent some more time defuzzing, and then he recognised the big man in denim sitting next to Catrin on a haybale. He was resting with his back to the wall, with his big hands behind his head and his legs jutting out in front of him. Lou could smell the leather of his footwear, big brown builders' boots with steel toecaps. Lou realised who he was.

'Big M,' he whispered through cracked lips. He was thirsty, very thirsty, and suddenly he was sick. He managed to wriggle sideways before he brought up the burger meal on the floor by the side of his bed, which rustled as he moved – it was made of straw.

They helped him outside, so that he could get some air, while Big M cleared the mess inside with a spade.

Lou sat on a bale by the door to the building, which was small and round and squat. There were two others, completing a circle, and they looked more like hobbit homes than anything else. Lou and his companions could be sitting by a settlement somewhere in Africa, or in the Indian desert. Big M sat on a nearby bale and observed him.

'They're made of woven straw plastered with mud, six more behind us,' he indicated with a thumb over his shoulder. 'Nice and warm, but you have to be careful with the candles, and there's a chance you'll wake up sharing your bed with a mouse,' he added nonchalantly.

Catrin was sitting on another bale, hunched in a posture which Lou knew well. She was upset.

'I'm sorry about this Manawydan, I never thought he'd do something like this.'

She appeared on the verge of tears.

'Hey, never mind, it wasn't your fault,' he replied softly. 'Little shits like this all over the place. I'm used to it.'

Lou resented being called a little shit, but there again he was one, so he kept quiet.

He was chattering with cold, but his insides felt better now. It was strange being so close to Big M, in the flesh; Lou had dealt with an abstract and far-away heroic figure for so long that the man had reached some sort of mythological status in his mind. Coupled with his size and his rugby exploits, he seemed totemic and special. And pleasant, too, really nice. Anyone else might have been abusive, or aggressive, but the man in front of Lou was calm and dignified and urbane, if a touch withdrawn or resigned.

Lou wondered if he should apologise. Was he ready for that sort of thing? Would it mean anything to anyone – or would it sound like so many of the century's empty mouthings, another fatuous apology?

Sorry all you little sardines, for putting you into tins...

'I'm sorry,' said Lou. He was talking to the ground.

'Sorry for what, exactly?' asked Big M.

Lou looked up into his eyes, blue and candid and clear. They held his gaze openly, inquiringly. He seemed genuinely interested in Lou.

'Sorry about the fields,' answered Lou. 'Don't know what got into me.'

Catrin got up, went over to him, and stooped down.

'And the rest too, tell him about the rest. He deserves to know the truth, Llwyd.'

But he was unable to answer and she regained

her seat. As they rested in silence, Lou gathered his thoughts. His eyes detected a faint light on the eastern horizon, and he realised that the dawn was approaching. The mice would be coming to the end of their shift now. Hundreds, maybe thousands of them, out there among the skyscraper stalks. Wizzing up and down in their invisible lifts, tiny furry citizens in their city of stems. They'd been around mankind for a long time, sharing his story; sharing his food and his home too. Perhaps they were the gods of old, made small. Perhaps that might happen to man too; he would be rescaled, cut down to size again in the ancient landscape. No bad thing, thought Lou. That would give the other animals a chance.

Maybe it would be easier to tell the whole story now, get it off his chest, clear the account. What was the point in dissembling any further anyway, playing a stupid game, messing with people. Wasn't it easier to be frank and straightforward?

He began to tell them about the background: his research, the threat posed by Dermot Feeney's book, academic competition, the race to shine in a field of excellence.

‘I wouldn’t mention fields of excellence right now,’ said Big M.

Again, Lou said sorry.

‘No point in saying sorry over and over again,’ said Big M, ‘just explain to me why you did it so that I can understand, that’s all I’m asking. You’ve just wiped out most of our winter store of food and I think we deserve to know why. Someone or other has had it in for us since we came here and we’ve just taken it every time, turned the other cheek, but now I really want to know what’s behind all this.’

Big M was perturbed, but not angry. He stood up and came to stand by Lou. He seemed very big, standing up to his full height, his close-cropped hair looking like stubble. His head was almost out of sight, he really was a huge man. How old was he? Lou tried to fix an approximate year but it was impossible, the man could be anything between thirty and a hundred. Some words came echoing out of the memory stick in his breast pocket. *I’m a sex god you know*. And yes, he was still very good looking, in a mature sort of way. He really did seem ageless.

Lou went through some of the reasons for his actions. But they didn't ring true. Sitting in the stalled car, earlier, a simple realisation had appeared in the full beam of his headlights. He'd tried to destroy Big M's story, not because he had anything against Big M, but because he was expressing his own sense of failure. He had known all along, inside himself, that he'd never been up to the task of writing a stand-out book about Big M. He simply wasn't up to it. He maybe had the acumen, he maybe had the intellect, but he didn't have the mental stamina or the dogged perseverance needed to write such a book. One needed intellectual slack to do such a thing. He had no depth, no intuition, no experience of probing and delving. His generation had never suffered, and unfortunately for mankind, most people became prescient and compassionate and accommodating only when they'd suffered a bit themselves.

'What I did, really, was a bit childish,' said Lou finally. 'The anger inside me was the anger of a child.

I wasn't trying to hurt you Big M, you seem to be a nice kind of guy. But I was angry because I saw other people being successful around me and I was getting nowhere. When you see another academic being praised and admired and honoured, and all the time you're sitting in your little room going nowhere, a little red monster enters you, pumps you full of envy and bile, you get hot and angry inside, you want to...'

Lou trailed off, knowing that he didn't need to say any more.

'And anyway, you provoked me,' he added. 'Why did you feed me the memory sticks, what was that stuff with the scarecrows, dressing them up like me?'

He looked round towards the other two; Big M had retreated to his bale and was sitting in his characteristic pose, lying back against the hut with his head resting in his hands. He'd found himself in this position many times over the last few years as various adversities had arrived.

'I have absolutely no idea what you're talking about,' answered Big M, and Lou knew immediately that he was telling the truth.

'And you, Catrin – was it you who did it?'

She looked aghast.

'Me? Why the hell would I do that, Lou? I'm about to give birth to your child, for God's sake. Do you think I've got nothing better to do than...'

She trailed off, and again Lou knew instinctively that she was telling the truth. So it had all been a co-incidence; paranoia and guilt had fed his imagination. As with most conspiracy theories, bigotry and ineptitude had been at the root of it all.

'So this is what an avenging angel looks like,' said Big M quietly. 'Are you my avenging angel, Llwyd? Are you the angel of the bottomless pit? Were you behind the gunshot at the hotel that night?'

Lou lifted his head, and allowed himself a smile. 'I had nothing to do with it, and you know it. You'll have to blame that on Pryderi. He got in with the wrong crowd, I'm not that type,' he answered.

'No, you're just an ordinary bloke, aren't you Llwyd,' said Big M, returning to his reflective head-in-hands pose. He was tired now, and feeling resigned again. Resigned to man's idiocies and petty squabbles.

'You know something, Llwyd,' said Big M quietly, 'man's reputation as an intelligent animal rests on a very few shoulders.'

Lou took a while to digest this.

'Not everyone can be famous you know,' continued Big M. 'I quite liked it in the Middle Ages when artisans were anonymous, just part of the team. I also liked it when we had small gods for everything; we may have been misguided, but having a god for the trees gave trees some safety and having a god for the rivers gave rivers some protection.'

Big M went off on a riff about the western cult of the self. There was no attempt now at graft or perseverance or a personal journey, he said. The only way to reach immortality was via a pair of plastic tits or three minutes of prancing about on X Factor. And what about the past? Why had Wales turned its back on its own history and adopted the fables of a small Mediterranean country, a land of sand and burning sun? Why had they welcomed a foreign god, singular and seductive, but all the same very human?

Lou kept quiet. The man wanted to have his say.

Let him rant. Let him put the world to rights. That's what old men did when they couldn't chase women or carouse any more...

Lou regarded the man uncomprehendingly. His size and obvious power created a mesmeric force-field around him. Lou had met only one man like him: a Russian cosmonaut, Colonel Alexander Volkov, hero of the Soviet Union, who'd spent a year circling the Earth in Mir when the USSR disintegrated, leaving him to watch from above, unable to return until someone at Star City paid the bills. He'd gone up a Soviet citizen and come down a Russian. Lou had met him at a university party when Volkov had been on a British tour, and like everyone else he'd been drugged by the man's presence. As everyone had agreed later, Volkov's mass had seemed different; he had his own forcefield, you could almost feel the magnetic rings pulsing around him.

The scene changed again as they sat there mutely. The dawn had established itself, but at the same time the atmosphere had become opaque and wispy. Soon they were sitting in a thick cool sea mist which muffled the world and erased the landscape below them.

'Oh bloody hell,' said Big M wearily. 'Not the sodding mists again. I thought they'd gone. I can't stand the thought of walking around in skimmed milk for another year.'

The birds and the animals, which had just started their morning chatter, fell silent again. Only the smash and swash of the distant sea serrated the silence, threading in and out of their white linen world.

'Look, a mouse,' said Catrin. She didn't fall into a panic, as she surely would have at home, thought Lou. Why was she different here?

The mouse was poised on the edge of a bale, sniffing the air, moving its uplifted head from side to side. Slowly, deftly, Big M moved his hand behind it and closed on it, then took it round for all to see. The mouse seemed unfazed; it sat in Big M's massive paw, looking at them unseeingly with dark, clear little eyes, its whiskers tremulous and hyperactive.

'Beautiful, isn't it,' said Big M. 'The harvest mouse, *Mycromys Minutus.* Makes a marvellous little ball of woven grass high among the corn stalks for its summer home.'

He turned it over gently and moved a finger aside, to show them its white belly. The rest of it was covered in a soft brown fur, tinted with russet.

'It'll take some of our seeds and store them in a winter larder underground. Isn't it wonderful?'

They admired it, snug in his hand, apparently unaware of its vulnerability.

Big M moved over to Lou's bale and sat beside him. Lou felt a warm, solid form press against him but detected no menace. Looking sideways towards Big M, he noticed the mouse tattoo on his chest, under his shirt on the left pectoralis major; the trademark badge of the old Welsh rugby teams. It looked faded and mystical; a warrior's scar, a man's story etched on his skin. Lou felt a pang of nostalgia for this other man's history; he heard the voices of a massed sepia crowd on the wind, and saw the blurred faces of his countrymen as they hurried in their thousands towards the field of battle. They were old or dead now, those people; their memories of

Wales had seeped away into the past.

'Open up,' said Big M, unfurling Lou's hand and transferring the mouse onto his palm before closing his fingers over the tiny body.

'There,' said Big M, 'what does that feel like? You're a god now Llwyd, you can do what you like with the mouse. Anything. You can kill it quickly, you can kill it slowly, or you can let it go. Up to you now Llwyd. Look how massive you are, how tiny it is. One movement from you and it's dead. You can decide its fate Llwyd, you have the power of life or death over it. Decide!'

Lou sat on his bale in the mist, with the beautiful little mouse in his closed hand. Such a nice warm feeling. He raised and flipped his hand round so that he could look directly into its face; again, the mouse seemed unperturbed, or at least resigned to its fate.

Two little mouse eyes looked into his, and they stayed like that for a minute or so as Lou examined the face and the quivering whiskers, the implausible little mouth.

'It's the acrobat of the wheatfields, swinging

through the corn stalks,' said Big M. 'It drinks from droplets of water on blades of grass. Such freedom. Such licence to roam and destroy our crops, but it takes only what it needs, Llwyd. It doesn't destroy for fun. Only man does that on a regular basis. So do it, kill it if you feel like it. Break its neck and throw it into the hedge. You're in control now Llwyd...'

Lou continued to look at the little face for a while, then he straightened his hand, lowered it to the ground, and opened it. The mouse stayed stock still for a few seconds, as if awaiting the rasp of the guillotine, then it vanished into the mist.

A round of gentle applause rippled behind Lou's back, and he turned to see a group of about twelve people ringed around him. They were smiling, and a couple had glistening eyes.

'There you are, Llwyd, now you know what it feels like to be a god. And you've learnt a lesson that all country children learnt in the old days – that the best feeling of all is to spare the mouse, to let it go,' said Big M. 'Don't you think so, Llwyd?'

As he spoke, two figures came looming out of the

mist, startling them. It took a few seconds for anyone to recognise them, because they weren't expected, then Big M leapt to his feet, saying: 'Pryderi! Rhiannon!'

Lou stayed silent, head bowed, his eyes still on the mouse's path to liberation, as the people around him embraced each other, clasped hands, cried, all those things you do when you're reunited with someone important to you after a long time. It was pretty emotional, figures moving in and out of the mist, throwing their arms around each other, filling the air with human feeling. They took a while to settle, then Big M introduced him to the assembly and told something of the story, beginning with the memory sticks and Lou's quest for academic fame. He didn't mention Lou's attempt to eradicate Big M.

With an obliterating mist chalking out their features, Lou was reminded of a school production of *A Midsummer Night's Dream*, in which he'd played the malign Puck; and here they were again at the play's ending, with Big M as Oberon the king of the fairies reunited with his queen Titania in her bower deep in the forest. It was uncanny.

Then, Big M asked one of the group to take Lou into one of the huts so that he could get himself together and prepare for whatever he was going to do next. And what was that? Go home, presumably, thought Lou, though his mind was blank. He hadn't a clue what might happen next. And he needed to know what Catrin was likely to do. Was she going to stay here? Should he insist that his wife accompany him home, with their unborn baby still inside her? He'd never done alpha male before, and it was probably too late now. They'd all laugh at him probably, so he'd have to beg her. But on the other hand he wasn't all that bothered if she stayed. She seemed happy with these people, and he sensed that their marriage was effectively over. He'd find someone else in no time anyway. The Polish cleaner perhaps, she could live in the attic.

'Show him my collection,' said Big M as Lou was ushered away. This time he was taken behind the hut where he'd lain earlier, to the centre of the settlement. He noticed that there were nine huts in all, grouped in threes: a sort of democratic round table of huts, since none was bigger or more prominent that the others. In the centre, however, there was a different structure: it was a tall square building, set on four stanchions so that the first floor was a good metre above the ground, leaving an open space underneath.

'That's to prevent the mice from getting in, and to allow a flow of air to dry the grain,' said his guide, a young man of about twenty-five, dark and lean. 'We were experimenting this year with native cereals – the first field you tried to destroy had einkorn in it, the second had spelt, so it looks like we'll have to rely on emmer this winter.'

Lou mumbled an apology as they climbed a flight of steps to the first floor.

'There's a viewing area above, and this is where we keep the crop,' he said, pointing to a pile of empty hessian sacks and a couple of full ones.

'We'll have to salvage what we can from the two furthest fields, you're lucky that Big M is an easy-going guy, the rest of us wanted to kill you.'

Lou felt miserable, but remembered his mouse deliverance and felt a bit better.

From the ceiling hung a festoonery of boots and shoes, including a couple of rugby boots.

'Big M's collection of footwear, it's a bit of a joke among us. That's the only place where they're safe, away from the mice. But Big M likes to have his tootsies well covered, he likes a bit of style in his life.'

They heard a shout from outside, so they joined the rest. The mist was clearing quickly and the air around them was warming. Wafts of wheaty smells and hedgerow vapours began to flow on the air. The landscape below them was clearing, and they all seemed to be relieved.

'Come into my hut Llwyd,' said Big M. 'I've got something to show you.'

They went inside one of the buildings, just the two of them this time, and sat down on facing bales. It was nice in there, with bunches of herbs hanging from the rafters and a drift of flower petals, mainly rose, on the floor between them.

It was a homely kind of place, sweet smelling and comfortable, with a couple of exquisite rugs hanging on the walls. In the centre, between them, was a low wooden table which held a large bowl filled to overflowing with fruit. In between the apples and pears and plums, Lou could see objects glinting in the growing light. He watched them, and wondered what they were.

'Memory sticks, Llwyd. Flash drives, whatever you want to call them. I think you know what they are,' said Big M. 'Take a closer look.'

He was sitting in his usual pose, with his feet resting on the table. He had changed into a pair of brightly coloured moccasins.

Lou dropped to his knees and shuffled up to the bowl. He dipped his hands inside it and picked up some of the memory sticks. They were all identical, pearly white with the same silvery innards as the green, red and blue sticks which had led him such a merry dance. He piled them up in his left palm and played with them, then raised his eyes towards Big M, who said:

'You tried to destroy me, Llwyd. Is that right?'

Lou returned his look.

'I wasn't really trying to destroy you, I was trying to kill off everybody else's version of your life so that only mine was left.'

'And then you'd get all the credit, right?'

'Yes, I suppose so.'

'Llwyd, you can murder people, you can kill them off, but you can't kill off their stories. It's impossible.'

Lou looked down at the memory sticks and wondered what was inside them. He had some sort of idea.

'How many versions of my life do you think there are?' asked Big M.

He answered his own question. 'Dozens, hundreds, thousands... there's a version of me for everyone I've met.'

Lou allowed the memory sticks in his hand to cascade slowly back into the bowl.

This time it was Big M who dropped to his knees and shuffled to the table.

He fingered through them, picking fruit out of the

way as he went, until he found one particular memory stick. He held it up to the light and grunted softly. Then he handed it to Lou.

'That's the one I like best. It's the most complete. I wrote it myself, actually. Of course, it could be the least reliable of all the versions. You yourself will have to decide on that.'

Lou held it reverentially and stared at its inner corridors. He imagined the treasures inside: the whole story, unexpurgated, warts and all. Big M's mythologial childhood, his great rugby days, his life afterwards as celebrity cook, comedian, style guru, all-round nice guy. Big M, the great giver of gifts, had probably given him the most valuable gift of all.

'You know Llwyd, it's actually much easier to be laid back and pleasant. It takes so much less energy, and you don't have to spend half your life looking for alibis or avoiding people. It really is better for everyone, and you get to enjoy life more. Why not give it a try?'

Big M was back in his familiar pose. He looked content, at ease with himself.

'It's yours if you want it, Llwyd.'

Lou's head jerked upwards, shocked.

'What, this?'

Lou held the memory stick in the air between them.

'Yes, my life story, complete. You can have it. Use that stick to write the story yourself. You can claim unprecedented access, original sources, the story as never told before...'

Lou began to splutter, but Big M waved aside his protestations.

'No Llwyd, don't bother with all that stuff. Just take it, do it. It's my present to you, but on one condition.'

Lou knew immediately what that was.

'Of course Big M, I won't destroy it, I won't mess around any longer. I'll play it straight, I promise.'

Big M sat still for a while, his eyes gleaming.

'We'll see, Llwyd, we'll see what you're really made of. And do you know something, Llwyd? You could actually change my story a bit. Every story is warped with time, even our own individual stories. In the old days this story would have ended with Catrin returning home with you obediently and living a rather sad life, never fulfilling herself. But you can give it a new ending, Llwyd. It's up to you and Catrin to change the ending, not to be helpless individuals swatted this way and that by the gods. Correction, it's up to the whole of the human race to sort it out now.'

'You sound as if you've given up,' said Lou.

'I haven't given up on life, but I've almost given up on humanity,' answered Big M. 'Anyway, when this project is up and running I'm thinking of retiring. I'll go back to Ireland, or maybe to the Isle of Man. That's where my family comes from, you know. Sea all around me, I need the sea. It's very important to me.'

'Why?'

Big M gave him a wry smile.

'Oh, I don't know. Wide open spaces? Mystery? Very few people? The sea's a huge sleeping monster. I like its power, its beauty.'

'You don't like people very much?'

'I like them individually, but as a mass they're so destructive. They're a plague, really. But they think they're gods. That's what mirrors are for, to remind them every day that they're gods.'

'And there aren't any real gods?'

Big M took off his moccasins and massaged his feet. After a while he looked up at Lou and said:

'You know that song about the three blind mice? My mother used to tell me a story about those mice when I was a kid. Bedtime story. She said the first mouse was a messenger from the vast plains of the North, at a time when there were many gods, gods of small things like rivers and trees. The mouse announced that all the small gods were going away and they would never return to Earth again, but that one of the gods would stay behind in the South, just in case...

'Then a second mouse came from the South and said that the sole god who'd stayed on Earth had become lonely and had decided to join the rest, but he'd left a mouse in the East to act as a messenger between himself and mankind...

'Then a third mouse came from the East and told the people of Earth that all the gods were dead, but they needn't worry because a fourth mouse would come from the West one day to save mankind...'

'And what does all that mean?' asked Lou, puzzled.

'Not really sure. Mum was a great one for stories. I think she was trying to warn me that humans are a race of fibbers who are constantly changing the story to suit themselves. God was the best alibi they ever invented. But Lou, they really do have to face up to their responsibilities now and realise it's up to them. No excuses.'

Big M replaced his moccasins, got up, and stretched.

'Anyway, that's enough moralising for now. That's another human minefield, preaching. Come on, let's join the rest of them.'

Lou walked along, thinking about their conversation. He really did mean it; he was sincere when he made his pledge to Big M. But then his mind clouded over when he thought about his promise to

Catrin about the baby and being a good father. Still, he really meant it this time.

They joined the rest of the group, who were still celebrating the return of Pryderi and Rhiannon. They looked different, more engaged and vital than the urbanites who usually milled around Lou. They were as sleek as the mice, more in tune with their surroundings.

A simple breakfast had been prepared and laid out on a table made of haybales. They were discussing the day's plans, how they'd try to save what they could of the crop, who'd do what. The woman called Rhiannon pointed to the world below them and said: 'Look, I can see the road again, and some walkers over there on the coastal path. People again!'

Lou left them and went to stand at the edge of the compound, trying to formulate some plans of his own. Below him the mist had cleared and the landscape had emerged extra sharp, clear and very beautiful. Fields stretched as far as the eye could see: there were countless vales with rivers between them; trees and hedges stitched together in a quilt of classical beauty. Lou felt very big and very small at the same time. He was a giant with a great story inside the miniature world of the memory stick, and he was also a midget in the rolling landscape of Wales. He might stay here himself, if they let him. If he could stand the country life. Town mouse, church mouse, country mouse. He'd probably scuttle back to brickwork eventually. Up to now he'd been a man who liked to gnaw his way through other people's walls, other people's cables. Perhaps it was time for a change. Time for a nice relaxing time in the country, a hammock slung between two trees, siestas in the afternoon sunshine. But there again, he'd have to work hard and that might not be quite so...

Lou turned round to see what the rest were doing. He swivelled, and held the scene in a long stare.

There was nobody there. Perhaps they'd gone down to the fields to start work. Perhaps they'd disappeared into the memory stick again. He had no idea, but he wanted to find them. In passing the breakfast bales he picked up a small, flat, freshly baked loaf, and took it with him as he started walking by the edge of the ripe corn, towards the second field. He tore off chunks of bread and ate them as he went, picking off blackberries and wild strawberries on the way. At some point he took his digital camera from a pocket and took a picture of the cornfield still standing, yellow under blue. It would be ideal as a screensaver if he went back to his college desk, to start all over again.

At some point he found himself calling, calling out a name.

'Manawydan... Manawydan...'

It was the first time he'd ever used his full name, unconsciously, without thinking.

In that moment, his lips red with blackberry juice, alone in the cornfield under a vast blue sky, he felt like a small child calling out to his father.

Third Branch of the *Mabinogion*: Manawydan, son of Llyr

After the seven men had buried Bendigeidfran's head at the White Tower in London, Manawydan sighed with sorrow. 'I am the only one who has no place to go,' he said.

His friend Pryderi then offered him the seven cantrefs of Dyfed, as well as his mother Rhiannon as his wife. Manawydan talked to Rhiannon; he was delighted and agreed to Pryderi's proposal.

With Pryderi's wife, Cigfa, they began a circuit of Dyfed, hunting and enjoying themselves; they had never seen a place better to live in, or hunt in, or more abundant in honey or fish and a friendship developed between the four of them. They began a feast at Arberth, but as they sat there they heard a tumultuous noise and a blanket of mist fell. The mist became bright, and when they looked they could see nothing at all where they had once seen flocks and herds and houses, only the desolate court and the four of them remained.

They wandered through the realm living on wild animals, fish and swarms of bees but after a year they grew tired and set off for England to seek a craft and earn a living.

They came to Hereford, where they began saddle-making. Their saddles were so fine the other saddlers wanted to kill them, but they were warned and Manawydan decided they should leave, although Pryderi wanted to stay and fight. In the next town they took up shieldmaking, but the same thing happened, and in the third, shoemaking, but the same thing happened again and they decided to head back to Dyfed.

Hunting on the way, their dogs found a gleaming white boar in a thicket and a huge fort, newly built. Pryderi went inside and saw a well with a golden bowl, but when he touched it his hands stuck fast and he couldn't leave. Rhiannon followed to find him, and she, too, stuck fast.

Seeing that she and Manawydan were alone, Cigfa despaired, but he swore he was a true friend. They tried their hand at shoemaking again, but their shoes were so fine the other shoemakers wished to kill them. So they took some wheat back to Arberth and settled there. Manawydan planted a field, then a second and a third. But when he came to harvest the first field, and then the second, he found them stripped bare. Keeping watch over the third field he saw a huge army of mice climbing the stalks and stealing the ears. He managed to catch one that was very fat and took it back to court.

He wanted to hang the mouse as a thief, but then a poor cleric approached, who begged him to stop: a priest followed and then a bishop. The bishop asked him to name his price to spare the mouse and Manawydan asked for the release of Rhiannon and Pryderi and for the enchantment to be removed from the seven cantrefs of Dyfed, and this was granted.

Manawydan still refused, asking to know who the mouse was. The bishop told him the mouse was his own pregnant wife and that he, Llwyd, had enchanted the land to avenge Gwawl, son of Clud.

Manawydan still refused to spare the mouse, until Llwyd promised there would be no more vengeance and he saw Rhiannon and Pryderi returning. Then he released the mouse who turned into a fair young woman. He looked around and saw all the land inhabited again, complete with herds and houses.

Synopsis by Penny Thomas
for the full story see *The Mabinogion, A New Translation*
by Sioned Davies (Oxford World's Classics, 2007).

Afterword

The original *Mabinogion* probably took centuries to form and coalesce, but I wrote this book very quickly, in a couple of months, and I really enjoyed the experience.

First I read the preceding books in this new Seren series, and I got something from all of them, though I particularly liked Niall Griffiths' boisterous contribution so I stole some of his sulphur for my own use. I like this idea of a modern take on the fables, though it directly contravenes the tradition of the Celtic storytellers, who told it as their grandfathers did, with no extra bits, in a formal and dignified manner. One factor I found especially interesting: were the contemporary authors looking towards the Old World as they wrote their stories, or towards the

New World? When I was a young man I was actively aware of the ties and the traffic between Wales and Ireland, and I was conscious of the Celtic countries' ancient (but never moribund) dance around each other, and around England too. I refer in my story to a special relationship, but not the arranged marriage between Britain and the US, rather the brotherhood between Wales, Scotland, Ireland, Cornwall and Brittany, created by blood ties and the resultant cultural connections. Of course America has long been important to Wales; at least eight presidents have had Welsh ancestry, but with the recent blooming of a global US pop culture via TV and the web it seems to me that American culture has swamped Britain and skewed the island's cultural axis, so that Celtica has faded from general consciousness, other than some woolly and romantic tosh seen on our screens, with the Potterisation of Merlin being a typical example. How many modern Britons have read that Irish classic *The Táin*? How many had delved into *The Islandman* by Tomás O'Crohan and Robin Flower, or *The Aran Islands* by J.M. Synge? How many of them have heard of Sorley MacLean or his quintessentially Celtic poem, 'Hallaig'?

The *Mabinogion* in general, and the third branch in particular, owes a great deal to Ireland, Manawydan himself coming from across the water. Originally a five-star sea god, he was made mortal by the Welsh and rendered as a clean cut nice guy, a Sean Connery figure who'd retired because he didn't want the aggro any more. In the American version George Clooney would be cast as a tired but still attractive ex-federal agent inveigled into one last assault on the Mob. He's still cool and he's still a fixer, but he wants to stay poolside with a tall drink and good company. This turn-the-other-cheek side to the Welsh Manawydan smacks of Christianisation, but I'm no expert.

Having written some pretty outlandish stuff in my time – I didn't realise how strange I was until I wrote a book – I decided to play it straight with this story, mainly because I was writing to commission and didn't want to let the side down. I would have loved to write it as noir or pastiche, and I think Malcolm Pryce would have had a field day, but I haven't his talent. So here it is, my version of the third branch. I feel privileged to be part of this venture, since I'm in pretty impressive company. I have tried to reflect the huge, unpeopled landscapes of prehistory – the space, the light, the silence, the epic time spans. I have also tried to reflect the Celts' fabled absorption with detail, as seen in their metal work and decorative artwork; the computer memory sticks in my story are the equivalent of decorated capitals in the *Book of Kells*. They also represent Irish, Welsh, and other influences on the Mabinogion myth cycle. I've told the story from the viewpoint of the 'baddie' and I've tweaked his motives for revenge; I hope purists will forgive me. Otherwise I've played it pretty straight. I have to admit that during the process I felt no fellow-feeling with the original storytellers, who would be appalled, probably, by the liberties I've taken.

This is a groundbreaking series and I congratulate Seren on their foresight; I'm surprised that the Welsh-language publishers didn't do it a long time ago. The Triads would be an obvious consideration.

And so finally I come to the Anglo-Welsh tradition, which I suspect is coming to an end in its present form, or at least entering a different phase. Maybe this series is a fitting epitaph to a century of English writing by people with deep roots in the Welsh tradition. How many people will write in both languages in future? We have only a handful now, and as our written culture splits quite clearly into Welsh writing and English writing in Wales, a new future beckons.

I hope you enjoy my book.

Lloyd Jones

GWYNETH LEWIS
THE MEAT TREE

A dangerous tale of desire, DNA, incest and flowers plays out within the wreckage of an ancient spaceship in *The Meat Tree*, an absorbing retelling of one of the best-known Welsh myths by prizewinning writer and poet, Gwyneth Lewis.

An elderly investigator and his female apprentice hope to extract the fate of the ship's crew from its antiquated virtual reality game system, but their empirical approach falters as the story tangles with their own imagination.

By imposing a distance of another 200 years and millions of light years between the reader and the medieval myth, Gwyneth Lewis brings the magical tale of Blodeuwedd, a woman made of flowers, closer than ever before: maybe uncomfortably so.

After all, what man has any idea how sap burns in the veins of a woman?

Gwyneth Lewis was the first National Poet of Wales, 2005-6. She has published seven books of poetry in Welsh and English, the most recent of which is *A Hospital Odyssey*. *Parables and Faxes* won the Aldeburgh Poetry Prize and was also shortlisted for the Forward, as was *Zero Gravity*. Her non-fiction books are *Sunbathing in the Rain: A Cheerful Book on Depression* (shortlisted for the Mind Book of the Year) and *Two in a Boat: A Marital Voyage*.

OWEN SHEERS
WHITE RAVENS

"Hauntingly imaginative..." – Dannie Abse

Two stories, two different times, but the thread of an ancient tale runs through the lives of twenty-first-century farmer's daughter Rhian and the mysterious Branwen... Wounded in Italy, Matthew O'Connell is seeing out WWII in a secret government department spreading rumours and myths to the enemy. But when he's given the bizarre task of escorting a box containing six raven chicks from a remote hill farm in Wales to the Tower of London, he becomes part of a story over which he seems to have no control.

Based on the Mabinogion story 'Branwen, Daughter of Llyr', *White Ravens* is a haunting novella from an award-winning writer.

Owen Sheers is the author of two poetry collections, *The Blue Book* and *Skirrid Hill* (both Seren); a Zimbabwean travel narrative, *The Dust Diaries* (Welsh Book of the Year 2005); and a novel, *Resistance*, shortlisted for the Writers' Guild Best Book Award. *A Poet's Guide to Britain* is the accompanying anthology to Owen's BBC 4 series.

RUSSELL CELYN JONES
THE NINTH WAVE

"A brilliantly-imagined vision of the near future... one of his finest achievements." – Jonathan Coe

Pwyll, a young Welsh ruler in a post-oil world, finds his inherited status hard to take. And he's never quite sure how he's drawn into murdering his future wife's fiancé, losing his only son and switching beds with the king of the underworld. In this bizarrely upside-down, medieval world of the near future, life is cheap and the surf is amazing; but you need a horse to get home again down the M4.

Based on the Mabinogion story 'Pwyll, Lord of Dyfed', *The Ninth Wave* is an eerie and compelling mix of past, present and future. Russell Celyn Jones swops the magical for the psychological, the courtly for the post-feminist and goes back to Swansea Bay to complete some unfinished business.

Russell Celyn Jones is the author of six novels. He has won the David Higham Prize, the Society of Authors Award, and the Weishanhu Award (China). He is a regular reviewer for several national newspapers and is Professor of Creative Writing at Birkbeck College, London.

NIALL GRIFFITHS
THE DREAMS OF MAX & RONNIE

There's war and carnage abroad and Iraq-bound squaddie Ronnie is out with his mates 'forgetting what has yet to happen'. He takes something dodgy and falls asleep for three nights in a filthy hovel where he has the strangest of dreams, watching the tattooed tribes of modern Britain surrounding a grinning man playing war games.

Meanwhile gangsta Max is fed up with life in his favourite Cardiff nightclub, Rome, and chases a vision of the perfect woman in far-flung parts of his country. But as Max loses his heart, his followers fear he may be losing his touch.

Niall Griffiths' retellings of two dream myths from the medieval Welsh Mabinogion cycle reveal an astonishingly contemporary and satirical resonance. Arthurian legend merges with its twenty-first century counterpart in a biting commentary on leadership, conflict and the divisions in British society.

Niall Griffiths was born in Liverpool in 1966, studied English, and now lives and works in Aberystwyth. His novels include *Grits*, *Sheepshagger, Kelly and Victor* and *Stump*, which won Wales Book of the Year, and *Runt*. His non-fiction includes *Real Aberystwyth* and *Real Liverpool*. He also writes reviews, radio plays and travel pieces.

HORATIO CLARE
THE PRINCE'S PEN

The Invaders' drones hear all and see all, and England is now a defeated archipelago, but somewhere in the high ground of the far west, insurrection is brewing.

Ludo and Levello, the bandit kings of Wales, call themselves freedom fighters. Levello has the heart and help of Uzma, from Pakistan – the only other country in the free world. Ludo has a secret, lethal if revealed.

Award-winning author Horatio Clare refracts politics, faith and the contemporary world order through the prism of one of the earliest British myths, the Mabinogion, to ask who are the outsiders, who the infidels and who the enemy within...

Horatio Clare is a writer, radio producer and journalist. Born in London, he grew up on a hill farm in the Black Mountains of South Wales as described in his first book *Running for the Hills*, nominated for the *Guardian* First Book Award and shortlisted for the *Sunday Times* Young Writer of the Year Award. Horatio has written about Ethiopia, Namibia and Morocco, and now divides his time between South Wales, Lancashire and London. His other books include *Sicily through Writers' Eyes*, *Truant: Notes from the Slippery Slope* and *A Single Swallow* for which he was the recipient of a Somerset Maugham Award.

FFLUR DAFYDD
THE WHITE TRAIL

Life is tough for Cilydd after his heavily pregnant wife vanishes in a supermarket one wintry afternoon. And his private-eye cousin Arthur doesn't appear to be helping much.

The trail leads them to a pigsty, a cliff edge and a bloody warning that Cilydd must never marry again. But eventually the unlikely hero finds himself on a new and dangerous quest – a hunt for the son he never knew, a meeting with a beautiful and mysterious girl, and a glimpse inside the House of the Missing.

In this contemporary retelling from Seren's New Stories from the Mabinogion series, award-winning writer Fflur Dafydd transforms the medieval Welsh Arthurian myth of Culhwch and Olwen into a twenty-first-century quest for love and revenge.

Fflur Dafydd is the author of four novels and one short story collection. She won the Oxfam Hay Emerging Writer of the Year Award 2009 and is the first female author ever to have won both the Prose Medal and the Daniel Owen Memorial Prize at the National Eisteddfod. She has also released three albums as a singer-songwriter and was named BBC Radio Cymru Female Artist of the Year in 2010. She lectures in Creative Writing at Swansea University and lives in Carmarthen with her husband and daughter.